THE ART OF MURDER

PARTNERS IN SPYING MYSTERIES: BOOK TWO

ROSE DONOVAN

Moon Snail Press

For Angelique

The Art of Murder

Copyright © 2023 by Rose Donovan

www.rosedonovan.com

Published by Moon Snail Press

Editing: Nicky Taylor Editing & Heddon Publishing

All rights reserved. No part of this book may be reproduced or transmitted in any form or by any means, electronic or mechanical, including photocopying, recording, or by any information storage and retrieval system without the written permission of the author and publisher.

All the characters in this book are fictitious, and any resemblance to actual persons living or dead is purely coincidental.

Cast of Characters at Serpentine Hall

Ruby Dove – Reading chemistry at Oxford. Designer and spy-sleuth on a mission to right colonial and fashion injustices.

Fina Aubrey-Havelock – Reading history at Oxford. Assistant seamstress to Ruby, and her best friend. Ready to defend Ruby at any cost.

Pixley Hayford – Shameless journalist on the hunt for a scoop. Always game for a Ruby and Fina adventure.

Sir Montague Dunbridge – Portrait artist, mentor, and host at Serpentine Hall with a larger-than-life presence.

Charles Vane – Mysterious yet familiar character, working for a sugar company from Barbados.

Luca Gatti – Owner of London's Finch Gallery, with a singular drive to succeed.

Flora Scott – Vivacious New York painter on the London arts scene, and collaborator with Ruby and Fina on a new show. Protégé of Sir Montague.

Gwendolyn Brice – Eccentric Welsh painter of promise and also a protégé of Sir Montague.

Dr Niall Rafferty – Dublin-born London psychotherapist dabbling in art therapies and other unknowns.

Helen Poole – Devoted secretary and housekeeper for Sir Montague. Devilishly efficient.

John Benbow – Loyal valet-cum-butler to Sir Montague. Served with him in the Great War.

Daphne Wandesford – Heiress to the Wandesford rolling-pin fortune, and a woman in search of liberation.

Tangerine – Flora's daring kitten with a flair for mischief.

Serpentine Hall

Billiard Room	Larder
Wine Cellar	Coal Room

Kitchen

Basement

Serpentine Hall

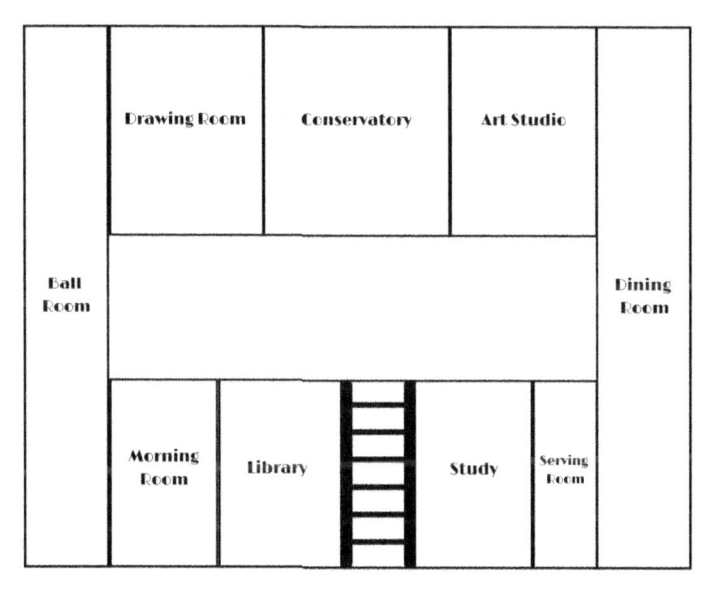

Ball Room	Drawing Room	Conservatory	Art Studio	Dining Room
	Morning Room	Library	Study	Serving Room

Ground Floor

Serpentine Hall

Black				Azure
Cobalt	Long Gallery			Indigo
				Magenta
Orange	White	Vermilion	Burgundy	Yellow	Burnt Umber	Viridian

First Floor

1

I tried to ignore it.

My gaze shifted, focusing on a watercolour dotted with tipsy Devon fishing boats. I sipped my wine and contemplated the canvas, mimicking the casual, insouciant manner of those around me.

"Intriguing, isn't it?"

The blond head of Luca Gatti, owner of this gallery on London's Finch Street, came into view. He pointed his glass an inch from the canvas. "One of our bestsellers. Not exactly daring, but better than the insipid paintings adorning most homes in England."

Suspecting the canvas hanging in my flat – a cheery portrayal of buzzing bees in a lush garden – was precisely that, I treated him to a non-committal "Mmm ..."

"You must be a keen observer of art, Miss Aubrey-Havelock." Luca waved his glass around the airy, light-filled gallery packed with murmuring people. "You've helped your friend Miss Dove birth such an artistic sensation."

Luca's wiry frame and sunken, pale cheeks leaned towards me earnestly, but his thin lips held a hint of irony.

"I appreciate the flattery," I said, "but I simply followed Ruby's instructions and stitched the silk onto the canvas."

Across the room, Ruby Dove – my best friend – raised a glass in our direction, showing off her crêpe de Chine crimson-and-navy frock. Her high-heeled red shoes, and black hair bunched into a curly bun atop her head, created a towering effect over her new friend and collaborator, painter Flora Scott. Unlike Ruby's statuesque build and calm demeanour, Flora's tiny frame exuded passion and energy. Waving her hands in a fluid, snaking motion, her arms glowed against the bright orange of her silk trouser suit. Presumably she was illustrating some complex artistic principle to Ruby.

"Regardless, the opening night is proving a wild success." Luca gestured towards the milling and burbling crowd, oblivious to the art on the walls.

Blast it. The distraction by the gallery door had returned. This time it was near the makeshift bar, a wobbly table jammed with half-empty wine bottles and stacks of highball glasses.

"Did you see that?" I asked.

Luca moved closer, sending a whiff of his aftershave in my direction. "Near the wine? Yes, I spotted someone moving about erratically. Perhaps I'll call on Joseph. He's standing outside, keeping watch over things."

"Perhaps not," I said above the vibrating hum from an ever-larger crowd in the gallery. "It will disturb the party."

Luca's mouth twitched with approval. "Quite right. Must not disturb the buyers."

"Why don't you walk around one side of the bar and I'll stroll around the other?" I suggested.

Luca agreed, ambling past a couple discussing my favourite piece in the show, a man and woman locked in an embrace. Mirroring the painting's movements, the man said, "No, no, they're quarrelling, darling. Notice her outstretched hand?"

The Art of Murder

The woman frowned. "They're dancing, William. Can't you see it?" She took her partner by the hand and he responded, twirling her around.

Onlookers flocked to the spontaneously waltzing couple, giving Luca and me the chance to move unnoticed behind the bar. Without warning, a petite woman in black trousers and a threadbare jumper popped up – much like the weasel in the children's rhyme – and dashed across the gallery, vanishing around the corner.

I sprinted after her, weaving through the thick undergrowth of the increasingly inebriated crowd. Dodging one glass flung near my face, I ducked more jutting limbs blocking my path.

But a grasping arm halted my progress.

"Fina Aubrey-Havelock, as I live and breathe!"

It was Daphne Wandesford, heiress to the Wandesford rolling-pin fortune. Despite her powerful grip on my arm, she tottered and swayed on her high heels.

"Where have you been, darling?" she queried, strands of her long blonde hair dipping into her champagne glass.

Experience told me to ignore Daphne's rhetorical questions. She'd soon dry up, and I couldn't have escaped her grip if I had tried.

"These paintings are fabulous! Now, do tell me. A little bird said you stitched the fabric onto the canvas. How clever of you," she fluted in a slightly strangled upper-class accent. Her pink arms shifted up and down like a voluptuous butterfly. "May I steal you for a teensy moment? I'll introduce you to an absolutely divine fellow, Niall Rafferty. Although we've just met, I'm certain you two will get on like a house on fire."

Finally jerking my arm free, I said, "Talking of a house on fire, I must dash!"

Her bangled arm jingled towards the ceiling. "Ah yes, the call of nature, darling. Or must you repair your make-up? You're terribly fetching tonight ..."

Leaving Daphne behind, I rounded the corner and spied my quarry outside the ladies' toilet.

At first, I thought that a crab canapé had simply disagreed with this mole-like woman's stomach. But she did not intend to use the smallest room, at least not for its intended purpose.

Her eyes alight with maniacal fervour, she held up a match in one bony hand. She gazed at it lovingly for a moment before she struck it against the door frame.

My concentration on her was complete; the gallery conversations receded into a background hum and the acrid match odour wafted away. Instinctively, I sensed that match was not going to light a cigarette.

Just as the flame reached her fingers, my quarry moved her other hand from behind her back, gripping a stick of dynamite.

2

"Stop!" I flung myself towards the woman in black.

With eyes bulging like a feisty Pekinese, she careened backwards, pushing open the door to the ladies' toilet. I misjudged my angle of attack and tumbled over her onto the floor, tipping over a rubbish bin as I fell.

She struggled up and disappeared back into the corridor, her limp dark-brown bob flapping like wings trying to lift her into the air. I was left behind, sitting in a heap of discarded tissues and rubbish. Ignoring the fetid odour, I rifled through the tissues and found her discarded matchbox.

But not the dynamite.

She hadn't taken the dynamite with her, attested to by her tight-fitting clothing. With dawning relief, I realised she must be fleeing the proverbial scene of the crime, rather than planning to detonate a bomb.

"Feens!"

Ruby stood in the doorway, her hands curled over her lips. "What happened? I saw you dashing through the crowd. Are you injured?"

"Find the dynamite!" I fumbled on the floor, sending tissues flying into the air.

"Dynamite?" Ruby crouched down and cocked her head. "Did you hit your head?"

"Not this time." My adventures with Ruby often involved me hitting my head. Or rather, someone else coshing it.

Ruby made no move to help me, so I stopped and stared at her. "I'm perfectly serious. Please hurry – we must find the stick of dynamite I spotted. That woman was going to blow up the gallery!"

"Did you mean this?" Between two fingers, Ruby held a long black candle with a trailing wick.

I blinked. "B-b-but ... I could have sworn it was dynamite."

Ruby brushed a wisp of hair from her eyes. "Well, at least we won't all perish in a fiery ball of flame."

She rose and held out a hand. "Come on. Let's find this mysterious woman."

On jellied legs, I took her hand and instinctively smoothed my unruly fringe, which was prone to stick up at the most inappropriate times. My stomach remained in tangled knots of embarrassment rather than fear.

How could I make such a ghastly error?

Sheepishly, I trailed a few steps behind Ruby into the gallery. Unaware of the drama in the women's toilet, guests merrily munched on tiny sandwiches and canapes.

Ruby glanced at me. "The black candle does rather resemble dynamite, and I appreciate you always trying to keep us safe, Feens."

"You're too kind," I sighed. "But my imagination is rather lurid."

"What's important is that our candle friend has vanished" – Ruby swiped a glass of fizz from a passing tray – "and we may continue the frivolities, undisturbed. The show is a smashing success, don't you agree?"

"Mmmm ..." I chomped on a chocolate-covered biscuit, soothing my jangled nerves.

Despite Ruby's calming words, my eyes still scanned the crowd for the woman in black. Luca Gatti stood with Daphne Wandesford near our largest canvas, featuring Daphne herself resplendent in a tight-fitting yellow gown and plunging neckline. In recounting the story of the portrait, Flora said that Daphne simply couldn't sit still or stop talking, so she'd resorted to painting Daphne fully dressed whilst she drifted off to sleep. True to form, Daphne was the one chatting, whilst Luca surveyed the crowd.

To Daphne's right, Flora Scott stood with her mentor, Sir Montague Dunbridge, the famous portrait painter. Flora squealed and her hands flew to her cheeks in girlish delight. Sir Montague bent over her, chuckling in a deep baritone, his chin lowering into his blue cravat. His tall, rangy appearance, flushed red cheeks, and natty sienna smoking jacket made him a most striking figure, even amongst the bohemian crowd.

"Selkies and kelpies," I muttered under my breath.

"What's the matter?" Ruby asked absently.

My nemesis had popped up again from behind an easel in the corner of the gallery. I padded towards her steadily with my arms outstretched. A sudden surge of anger propelled me forward at a running clip.

When she was a few steps out of my reach, she simply pranced across the floor towards Sir Montague and Flora.

"Flora!" I pointed at my nemesis.

"Fina?" Flora whipped her head around, sending her long, elegant earrings smacking into her cheeks. "What the—?"

Before Flora could utter another word, my nemesis had

grasped another blasted black candle and lit it. She must have hidden her bag of supplies near the easel.

She jerked the candle high in the air, recalling a postcard my cousin had sent me of the Statue of Liberty.

"Ladies and gentlemen," she called in a surprisingly loud voice, softened only by the tinge of a lilting Welsh accent.

A silence blanketed the crowd, only to be broken by the tinkling of glasses smashing to the floor. Mouths gaped open everywhere, and a few guests shrank back into the shadows. I, too, found the long, flickering black candle singularly disconcerting. Peculiar how such a mundane item could become so menacing.

"This gallery opening is a farce."

Her words hung in the air, leaving only enough space for a low rumble from the crowd. Someone whispered, "Sweetie, it's Gwendolyn Brice! The portrait painter, who had a show here last year."

Gwendolyn's monologue continued. "You're all enjoying this young artists' exhibition, which is indeed a worthy cause. But a fraud lurks among you."

Luca held up a hand, jerked it down, and thrust it up again. "Miss Brice, I'd be delighted to discuss your concerns in private."

Gwendolyn's eyes narrowed. "You'd like nothing more than that, wouldn't you?"

She spun round and pointed a long, white finger at the tiny brown figure in orange.

"Flora Scott is a fraud."

Titters spread like Cornish rain on a summer's day.

Gwendolyn frowned. Clearly, this was not the reaction she desired; this scandalous news had positively thrilled everyone.

Her voice rose. "Flora Scott stole my painting. I demand a public apology, as well as the full restoration of my rights to the portrait."

This lapse into officious language only amplified the nervous whispers.

Still holding the candle high, Gwendolyn strode towards Flora's painting of an older woman stroking a cat. "This is my painting, not Miss Scott's."

The candlelight nearly singed the cat's whiskers.

"Though Miss Scott and I were under the tutelage of Sir Montague Dunbridge in Paris at the time," she said, "I painted it, not her."

Ruby caught my arm in the crowd's rush towards the portrait. "It's not Gwendolyn's. Look at the signature," she whispered in my ear. "Besides, it's Flora's most famous painting – how she gained notice from the London art world."

Puzzled faces turned towards Flora and Sir Montague, who stood agape at this spectacle.

Taking a small step forwards in her black ballet flats, Flora spoke first. Most petite women would have worn heels, but Flora revelled in her energetic ability to twist and turn at a moment's notice. Wearing ballet flats was an innovation, and one in keeping with the always-moving character of Flora Scott.

"First, let me welcome you to our exhibition, Miss Brice. Your presence means a great deal to me." Flora's soft American accent lacked the nasal tone of other New Yorkers. Her years in France, Italy, and England had smoothed the sharp edges of her twang.

"For those who don't recognise our friend," Flora said, "this is Miss Gwendolyn Brice, the famous portrait artist. And we did indeed hone our craft together under the sharp eye of Sir Montague Dunbridge."

Sir Montague closed his eyes and gave a slight bow.

"I am confused by your claim to this painting, Miss Brice," said Flora. "She was a most memorable subject – a Mrs Marchand – who passed away a few years ago." Her eyes crinkled at the corners. "And I believe the cat in the painting, Choco, went to live with a neighbour."

Gentle laughter rippled through the crowd.

"You always did give a pretty speech," said Gwendolyn. "But what you've omitted is that whilst you did paint a portrait of Mrs Marchand, I did as well. We left both our canvases with her because she planned to gift the portraits to her daughter."

"And did you speak to her daughter?" A slight impatience had crept into Flora's voice.

"Of course. The daughter never received the painting, and the original canvases could not be found."

Flora shrugged. "It means nothing. Paintings are lost all the time."

"I spent months searching for it, and nothing surfaced. So why don't you just admit it? You stole my painting," said Gwendolyn.

With crossed arms, Flora took a few swaggering steps towards Gwendolyn.

Sir Montague clinked a fork against his wine glass, halting Flora in her tracks. "As we may all gather from this sparkling debate, the authorship of this painting cannot be settled at this moment. Indeed, according to Miss Brice's story, we may never know the truth."

He quelled everyone's rising excitement with a downward thrust of his enormous hands. Clearly taken by a brainwave, his thick eyebrows shot upward.

"Therefore, I propose a contest."

The gallery exploded into pandemonium. Lightbulb flashes lit up the space, as if Fleet Street journalists had caught a whiff of a story and rushed into the gallery. Gwendolyn's flickering candle looked rather pathetic by comparison.

Sir Montague clapped three times. "I propose that Miss Brice and Miss Scott join me at my home on Cutmere Perch Island in

Cornwall. There, they will each paint someone of their choosing. They will also each invite two judges to decide which of the paintings is better."

In a moment of sobriety, Daphne Wandesford raised her hand. "If they each select two judges, won't it result in a deadlock?"

"Possibly. Therefore, as a mentor to these fine artists, I will break a tie, should one occur. Naturally, the judges must not be relatives of the painter, and they must have experience in the art world."

"How will the contest determine who owns the disputed portrait – and who is the true creator of it?" asked Flora.

"Whoever wins shall claim the portrait. But both you and Miss Brice must agree to this in the presence of these witnesses."

He turned to Flora.

"What say you?"

"I agree." Flora's voice deepened. "I will relish the challenge."

Gwendolyn stared at her black brogues, brows furrowed and a fist at her cheek.

She raised her head. "I agree."

Sir Montague lifted his hands as if he were welcoming everyone into his home. "Wonderful. That's settled, then. Both of you will now select your subjects for the portrait sittings."

"What? Here? Now?" asked Flora.

"As for the judges," continued Sir Montague, "you will have ample time to forward their names to me after this splendid opening concludes."

Flora rushed towards us and grasped Ruby's arm. She held up both their arms, locking them together like prize fighters.

"My partner in this exhibition, Miss Ruby Dove, will be my muse."

"Marvellous," cheered Daphne, breaking into applause. Others followed, and the gallery was soon awash with clapping.

As the applause died away, all eyes fell on Gwendolyn. A stab of empathetic pain jabbed my stomach.

But Gwendolyn was unfazed, her eyes slowly scanning the room as if searching for both an escape and a victim. Then her thin lips curved upward in a smirk.

Without hesitation, she stepped forward. Though the crowd had swallowed her small frame, her steady voice broke through the murmurs.

"That's my muse."

The crowd parted, though I wished they'd have remained in place. It would have been better for everyone.

Across the gallery, Gwendolyn Brice had her arm outstretched as if she were beckoning everyone to the promised land.

Her face illuminated with malicious glee, she aimed her forefinger at my forehead.

3

"Taste the delicious salt air, darlings." Daphne Wandesford clasped her chest and inhaled.

I wiggled my nose and handed the boatman my suitcase. "I followed Daphne's advice on the ferry from Penzance," I murmured to Ruby, "and the upshot was a queasier stomach from the seaweed odour."

"What was that, dear Fina?" Daphne's long eyelashes blinked under her enormous floppy hat, one more appropriate for the South of France in summer than spring in Cornwall.

But Daphne's gnat-like attention span rescued me from replying. She was now eyeing herself in a large silver compact, primping her long hair and pouting her lips in the tiny mirror.

A determined cloud hovered over us in the otherwise blue sky, adding to my already sour mood. During our three-hour ferry journey from Penzance to St Mary's in the Scilly Isles, the mercurial Cornish weather had treated us to sun, rain, and wind. Knowing what was in store, I'd chomped a hefty cheese scone as stomach insurance before we'd left Penzance. Though I was peckish now.

With her uncanny mind-reading ability, Ruby rummaged in

her capacious handbag and held up a gold-wrapped chocolate bar. She broke it into pieces and handed the paper around to everyone aboard the aptly named *Cutmere Away*. By the looks of Mr Tremore and his creaky craft, the boatman had been running this ferry from St Mary's to Cutmere Perch for decades. His grey whippet stood at the helm, ready to guide us towards our destination.

"Rascal, that's it," growled Mr Tremore. The dog scrambled onto a small blanket near the wheel. "Don't feed him no chocolate. Will hurt his stomach, it will."

"Never fear, Mr Tremore," I said. "Chocolate is my drug of choice, and as adorable as Rascal is, I won't be sharing it with him."

Behind me, Flora Scott hopped over the breach between the pier and the boat. "Whew. What a long trip. I'll be glad to settle in and start painting soon."

She gave me a sidelong glance. "Say, I didn't ask how you feel about becoming Gwendolyn's muse." The word held a naughty tinge, as if Gwendolyn had a lascivious intent in drawing me into her artist's lair.

I ignored her tone. "Travelling with Ruby is always a welcome adventure."

Flora surveyed Ruby, who was listening to Daphne's litany of dramatic trivialities. "How so?" asked Flora. "I haven't known Ruby long, but she strikes me as conscientious. Ambitious, yes. Thrill-seeking, no."

A gull cocked its head and eyed my bag speculatively, moving one webbed foot towards me. I pulled my bag in closer, weighing my next words. "Well, she has a knack for attracting adventure. Something intriguing always happens when we're together." I failed to mention this "something intriguing" was usually murder. And our own subversive activities, of course.

Worried that I'd overstepped the mark, I put in, "Besides,

how could I say no to Gwendolyn? And to you? Especially in front of everyone at the gallery."

Ruby leaned over. "Feens is putting on a brave face. She'd rather be at home with a cat at her feet, a cup of tea in her hand, and a good mystery or history book to read."

Flora's face softened. "You love cats too? I can't wait to see my sweet kitten, Tangerine. He's my good luck charm."

"Was there a kitten at your flat?" said Ruby. Ruby's feelings towards cats were tepid at the best of times. But she had made a recent exception for Pasty, an adorable grey cat who came with her new cottage along the Oxford canal.

"No, you didn't see Reen. That's his nickname."

"Where is Reen now?" My eye roamed about the boat, expecting a cat to mew from a hidden basket.

"Helen, Sir Montague's housekeeper, already brought him to Serpentine Hall."

"It's an unusual name," I said. "Is it named after the Cornish serpentine rock?" We'd passed a jewellery shop in Penzance featuring the dark-green stone.

"The original owner was a reclusive serpentine magnate who lived on the island year-round. Sir Montague lives there from late spring to early autumn," said Flora. "And it's the only house on Cutmere Perch."

"It must be impossible to ferry supplies in winter," said Ruby.

Mr Tremore lifted another case into the boat. "Aye, that it is. Even now, it's too early. But the gentleman never asked me my opinion, he didn't."

The warm sun on my face vanished and a sharp wind stung my cheeks. "I expect his housekeeper will have plenty of stores," I said. "Tell me about her."

"Helen Poole is the most efficient woman on God's green earth." Flora's eyes looked from side to side. "And I might be wrong, but she hopes to hear wedding bells soon. It would be impressive if she did ensnare Sir Montague. After all, he's never married, despite leaving a trail of broken hearts behind him."

"You're such a gossip, Flora," teased Ruby.

Flora cracked a rather sinister smile. "It pays, my dear, it pays."

She straightened and said casually, "But I'm sure Helen has enough tea and biscuits to weather any storm. Emotional storms or otherwise."

Ruby chuckled. "We eat things other than tea and biscuits, my American friend."

Daphne stopped her one-sided conversation with Luca Gatti, who Gwendolyn had named one of her judges.

She edged closer to Ruby and withdrew a sandwich in brown paper from her bag. Encircling the bulging bread with her hands, she tore into it and chewed with gusto. "We ought to eat whatever we choose whenever we choose."

Daphne moved her hand onto Ruby's knee. There might be more to her statement than a simple love of food.

But a familiar voice disrupted my musings.

"I say, gripping grub. This sounds like my kind of voyage."

4

"Pixley Hayford!"

I threw my arms around my friend's stout, muscular frame. "What on earth are you doing here?"

"Pix!" Ruby clasped Pixley's arm. "How lovely to see you!"

Pixley removed his trilby from his smooth, bald head and held it to his chest with a little bow. "At your service, madam. Your intrepid journalist friend has journeyed from the wicked metropolis to this forsaken Cornish outpost to snatch a story."

Ruby patted the bench. "Join us and tell us all about it."

Pixley hopped into the boat like a sprightly robin. He had accompanied Ruby and me on many adventures, and it was a relief he'd be with us this weekend. You could always count on Pixley.

"You must have known we were travelling to Cutmere Perch," I said. "It's too much of a coincidence."

"I confess, dear lady, that you're absolutely correct." With one finger, he pushed up his round, black-framed spectacles. "To my everlasting shame, I even shadowed you on the Penzance ferry. The temptation to surprise you was too great."

"How did you persuade your editor to send you?" asked Daphne.

"Have you two met before?" Flora looked from Daphne to Pixley.

"Aye," said Pixley. "We travel in the same circles." He held his nose high and affected an exaggerated posh accent.

"You are a one!" Daphne chuckled into her scarf.

"Once I got wind of this assignment, I used my excessive charm to persuade my editor to pay all my expenses to Cutmere Perch. At first, he planned to send another chap, but once I explained my intimate knowledge of a few players," he said, tapping my knee with his newspaper, "he agreed readily."

"Any noteworthy news?" I asked. "I haven't read the newspaper in two days."

He unfolded it. Mimicking a newsreel announcer, he intoned, "'Questions in Parliament over Italian Bombing of Harar', 'Cambridge wins Eighty-Eighth Boat Race', and 'St Lucia Coal Loader Strike Hits Britain'."

"Ugh." Flora's nose twitched. "That's why I never read the news. It's an evil world and I don't need any reminders of it."

"Not good for business, either." Until now, Luca Gatti had remained quiet, focusing his intense gaze on the horizon. Assuming he was warding off impending seasickness, I'd left him alone.

"Ah," said Pixley, "but here's good news: the Hindenburg airship made it to Brazil. Can you imagine a transatlantic crossing in a fantastic balloon?"

Luca sniffed. "Would be an improvement over this dingy dinghy."

"Rubbish." Daphne spread her hands wide. "It's perfectly atmospheric, darlings!"

And with that, we pulled away from the pier. Away from the picturesque harbour with its bobbing boats, ice-cream parlour, candyfloss, and racks of yellowing postcards, into the open ocean. Seagulls screeched overhead with fiendish delight. Rascal dashed forward like a bowsprit on a pirate ship, his ears flapping as the boat gained speed.

The sharp wind drowned out everyone's voices, giving me time to survey the party travelling to Cutmere Perch. Luca sat in the boat's stern with arms crossed, his determined, unnerving blue eyes peeking out from beneath a serviceable brown knitted cap. He was an intriguing and bizarre choice of a judge for Gwendolyn. After all, Gwendolyn had disrupted a show at his precious gallery. Why had he agreed to the position, and why did she think he'd vote in her favour?

I turned my gaze on Daphne in her inappropriate but fabulous camel-hair coat and white heels. And a floppy hat, of course. Despite her modest origins, the Wandesford rolling-pin fortune enabled Daphne's lavish travelling lifestyle among wealthy circles. At least she had put her inheritance to use as Flora's patron.

Small swells rocked the boat as we travelled further out to sea. My stomach lurched, so I tried to focus on the horizon. But I soon grew distracted.

The wind sharpened and Flora pulled her white headscarf closer to her powder-blue, full-length coat. She was unperturbed by the rocking of the boat, patting and playing with Rascal as his long snout probed each passenger. Her steady nerves would certainly be needed for the contest this weekend. Ruby had said Flora had a thick skin after being rejected so many times in the art world, sometimes because of her art, and sometimes because of skin-colour prejudice. Flora was also competitive, even ruthless, in her drive towards success.

"There she is," bellowed Mr Tremore, pointing just above the white horses foaming cheerfully ahead of us.

"Cutmere Perch," he said, with a mixture of awe and grim satisfaction.

The boat slowed, and a green, sloping island appeared over the crest of a wave. Scrub covered the flat western end, and the east slowly disappeared into a grass-covered hill overlooking the open sea. A sprawling, two-storey Georgian stone mansion stood on the hill, with two long wings flanked by a few scattered stone buildings. Serpentine Hall rose from the rock, staying low to the ground like a troll emerging into the light.

A sharp ray of sunlight ricocheted off the windows of Serpentine Hall in the otherwise darkening sky. As we approached, a few figures waved from the front of the mansion. Only Sir Montague's tall frame and elegant gait were recognisable.

To the left, a crumbling stone house came into view on the island's western edge.

"Is that house inhabited?" I asked.

Flora squinted. "If it's the old pest house, the answer is a definite no."

Pixley turned, hand gripping his trilby in place. "Pest as in pestilence? Fancy that. I've seen pest house ruins near London, but I'd never have guessed they'd be in Cornwall."

"When I visited Sir Montague last year, he spun quite a yarn about it," said Flora. "During a lesser-known plague in the fifteen hundreds, any ships docking had to quarantine here first. Unfortunately, the doctor from London overseeing the operation died from the disease, too."

Pixley hugged himself. "Glad we'll be in much warmer quarters soon."

Our boat halted alongside a small pier jutting from the shore. Rascal scrambled up onto the creaking wood slats, his owner in tow.

"Cutmere Perch," said Mr Tremore, as if he were a train

conductor announcing a station where no one was likely to disembark. "Everybody out. I'll help with the cases."

I heaved a sigh of relief as the visions of a glorious lunch at Serpentine Hall might soon become a reality.

"Feens," said Ruby, "what's the matter? Are you worried?"

"Just relieved to have arrived."

"Me too. A hot bath wouldn't go amiss."

"Followed by a large snifter of brandy," said Pixley. He gave me a little punch in the arm. "Though I expect Red might prefer more solid sustenance." Pixley was the only person who called me Red, given my cheeks' tendency to flame scarlet.

I waited until everyone had exited, playing with Rascal as he jumped back and forth between the boat and the jetty. Only Luca also stayed behind.

When it was my turn, I stepped on the bench, my low-heeled shoes wobbling. But the boat remained steady. That is, until an unexpected wave hit it, sending me swaying and the boat veering out from the jetty.

Mr Tremore stuck out his large, weather-beaten hand.

I grasped his fingers whilst watching the boat glide back towards the jetty. If the boat hit the jetty and stayed put, I'd be able to bridge the gap.

If it stayed put.

The seagulls screeched overhead, mocking my human attempt to use feet instead of wings.

The boat hit the jetty, and I waited to ensure it would not veer out again.

"I'm right behind you, Fina." Luca's fingers brushed against my back. "Don't worry. I'll catch you if you fall."

5

All eyes were watching me from the jetty. At least it felt that way. And becoming a spectacle only made my balance worse.

I raised my foot over the breach.

Quite literally out of the blue, another wave crashed against the boat. My foot slipped on a piece of seaweed and I tumbled down between the jetty and the boat, plunging into the icy, mud-coloured sea.

I gasped and spluttered, waving my arms about. I couldn't catch my breath. The shock of the cold seawater had seized my chest, and the tangy saltwater caught in my throat.

The deafening sound of seawater filling my ears soon muffled the cries of surprise and barking coming from the jetty.

My heart thumped, and I struggled to calm myself.

Breathe, Fina, breathe.

But every time I opened my mouth wide for air, in rushed saltwater.

Something banged my forehead and shoved itself into my neck. I grasped it in a fury, soon realising it was an oar handle. Holding tight now, I caught my breath and looked up, blinking through my wet hair.

"That's it, miss. Hold on and we'll get you out, we will," said Mr Tremore.

He leveraged the oar against the jetty like a seesaw, lifting me from the water and into the air, guiding me in an arc towards safety. Once I touched the edge of the jetty, Pixley and Ruby pulled me, heaving and panting, onto the wooden planks. I landed with a loud smack, as if they'd just caught the largest fish in the sea.

"Fina!" screeched Daphne, though her voice held pleasure in this dramatic scene.

A hand reached down and brushed the hair from my face.

"Is anyone a doctor? Who has medical training?" Pixley said from far above.

Someone gave me a terrific wallop on my back, sending a gushing river of seawater from my mouth.

"There now." A pleasant West Country burr soothed my nerves. "She'll come to in a minute."

I hoisted myself on two arms, staring at the concerned faces huddled around me.

"I-I-I'm so sorry," I babbled.

"Let me help you, miss," came the same voice.

A warm smile spread across the broad, pock-marked face, scored with years of laugh lines. "Name's Benbow, miss. John Benbow. Sir Montague's valet-butler, or whatever you choose to call me." He adjusted the brown tie on his grey suit and scooped up my case.

Pixley caught my arm and hauled me up.

"Here, Feens." Ruby removed her coat and draped it around me.

Pixley glanced over his shoulder at our group on the jetty. "Fina will be fine once she puts on warm clothes."

He piloted me up the steps, right behind Ruby, Flora, and the lumbering Mr Benbow.

Mr Benbow's voice floated down to us. "Ah yes, you and Miss Aubrey-Havelock are the students from Oxford. You're reading chemistry and she's reading history. You're also a fashion designer, I understand." He said "fashion designer" as if it were a rare bird species.

"Spot on, Mr Benbow. You are most well informed," Ruby replied. "Though Fina and I are here for the painting contest."

Mr Benbow snorted. "A right daft idea if you ask me, but then Sir Montague always did like parlour games."

"Who else is here?" asked Ruby.

"Well, besides Miss Helen Poole, a Dr Niall Rafferty is here. I believe Miss Flora Scott invited him."

"Niall's simply heaven on a stick." Daphne's voice echoed from the front of our procession. "He was at the ill-fated gallery opening, too."

"Niall is a psychotherapist," said Flora, "specialising in a new technique using painting to uncover past traumas. He'll be my second judge, my first being Daphne, of course."

"Darling, I shall delight in my closed-door deliberations with Niall," Daphne tinkled. "Though I already have those delicious painting sessions with him."

Mr Benbow coughed. "The last member of the party is a Mr Charles Vane. He and Mr Gatti will be judges for Miss Brice."

"Who's he?" asked Pixley.

"Can't rightly say," said Mr Benbow. "Someone with some company or other in the Caribbean. Now was it a sugar company? Miss Poole should have the particulars. She knows everyone."

"Hmm ... the Caribbean and sugar. What's the connection to the art world?" asked Pixley.

"Can't rightly say, Mr Hayford."

We stood overlooking the circular front drive of Serpentine Hall. Up close, the two low wings of the glowing stone house seemed to enfold us in the warm light. But the illusion was momentary, shifting from an embrace to a closed-in feeling as the pale light became grey.

I turned around and spotted St Mary's in the distance. The sight calmed my nerves, despite my still-shivering state. In the boat, I'd felt untethered from reality, but imagining people going about their daily lives a few miles away was a soothing balm against the loneliness of this tiny Atlantic island.

Pea shingle crunched underfoot as we neared the main entrance. Flanking the sides of the door were two serpents carved from greenish rock, each wound around a lighthouse they were about to devour.

Mr Benbow gave me a slow, bovine grin. "Those snake creatures won't bite, miss. The millionaire who owned this house thought it would be smart to have these fierce serpents guarding Serpentine Hall."

"But wasn't it named after the rock, not serpents?" asked Pixley.

"You're almost right, sir. The rock is called 'serpentine' because it resembles snakeskin." Mr Benbow patted one of the angry heads. "When Sir Montague bought the hall from that serpentine millionaire, the first thing he did was try to remove these fellows. But nothing would shift 'em from that spot. Obstinate as oxen, so they're here to stay."

Mr Benbow turned and began to arrange the mountain of cases, carefully setting each one next to the other as if he were lining them up for inspection.

Flora and Ruby had already entered Serpentine Hall, engrossed in discussing an esoteric fabric-dying process.

Pixley squeezed my shoulder, bidding me to stop.

"I'm freezing." My teeth chattered. "Did you want to tell me something?"

He lifted his chin towards the retreating figures, soon swallowed up by the imposing door.

"Let's stay away from prying ears," he whispered.

"Can ears pry? Never mind. Spill the beans."

"That's just it – you were spilt into the water."

"I'm perfectly aware of my fall into ignominy, thank you very much," I said.

"No, no. You misunderstand. You didn't fall into the water on your own."

"What, are you saying Rascal made me do it?"

Pixley's cherubic face turned grave. "No, Red. I wish it were the case. That cove – is he the gallery owner?"

"You mean Luca? The one in the dreadful knitted hat? He was trying to help me."

A loud plopping sound came from the sky. I looked at one of the poor serpents, his face now smeared in white seagull droppings. The seagull had just missed me.

"On the contrary, my dear Red," said Pixley. "I'm afraid Mr Gatti pushed you into the sea."

6

Piece by piece, I stripped off my wet, clinging clothes. With every item I removed, the cold terror of my ordeal faded into an unreal past, made improbable by the crackling flames in the grate. Whilst Serpentine Hall was a draughty old pile, a ferocious fire had warmed my room.

I patted my hair with a towel, mulling over Pixley's story. Pixley's spectacles might have slipped, creating the illusion that Luca pushed me into the water. Besides, why would he do it? What was there to gain?

A knock came at the door. "It's me," called Ruby.

"Come in. I'm behind the dressing screen."

Her swift footsteps echoed across the wood floor. "I found your green frock and woollen tights in your case. Will that do?"

"Perfect. Those tights are exactly what I need." I wriggled my frozen toes. "I'd forgotten how refreshing spring can be in Cornwall."

"Especially if you fall into the sea." She flipped the clothes over the canvas-stretched screen.

"Didn't Pixley tell you?" I asked.

"Tell me what? He started chin-wagging with Daphne as

soon as we arrived."

"Well, I'll tell you. Pixley saw Luca push me into the water."

Ruby was silent and then licked her lips. "If Pixley said he witnessed it, I believe him. His keen eye is second only to yours."

I glowed at the compliment.

"But why would he push you?" Ruby asked. "He doesn't strike me as a prankster. Quite the opposite: he's utterly single-minded and focused."

"On what? Art?"

"I mean single-mindedly ambitious. Don't you have the sense he always sleeps with one eye open?"

"He sounds like a smuggler or a pirate."

She laughed. "This is Cornwall, after all."

I pulled the frock over my head and smoothed my frazzled auburn fringe in the looking glass. Brushing it helped, but only a trifle. Since I had resembled a drowned rat a few moments before, I supposed it was an improvement.

"You may be right about Luca," I said. "Perhaps he was trying to steady me, but it appeared to be pushing?"

A tooth-tapping sound floated over the screen, a sure sign Ruby Dove's grey cells had shifted into gear.

Another tapping followed, this one more insistent.

"Someone's at the door," said Ruby.

The door creaked open, and I heard Ruby introduce herself. The honeyed, dulcet voice of Helen Poole responded. Her cut-glass accent drew my attention, though perhaps I ought not to have been surprised. After all, hard economic times meant many wealthy and titled people had taken positions worse than a famous artist's housekeeper. My cousin Lucy had just such a tumble down the social ladder, though it turned out that raising sheep suited her better than memorising the correct form of address for a widowed duchess.

Moving from behind the screen, I slid across the smooth

floor in my tights towards a woman closer to forty than thirty. She wore an emerald-green skirt, top, and cardigan, what Coco Chanel had dubbed a "twinset". But Miss Poole's elegant clothes halted at feet encased in sensible brogues. A dark-brown hank of hair draped over one side of her face, covering her left eye. In an incongruent gesture, she stuck out a rigid arm like an American businessman ready to agree on a deal.

"Welcome to Serpentine Hall, Miss Aubrey-Havelock. I was just telling Miss Dove it's customary to offer guests a tour – if you're well enough after your accident."

"How generous," I said, ignoring Miss Poole's invitation to discuss my ordeal. "I expect we're both most eager to explore."

"Lunch will be served shortly, so we'll have an abbreviated tour." We stepped into a long corridor lined with artistically mismatched rugs on the floor and a similar variety of paintings along the wall, from old ancestral portraits to Cornish landscapes to unemotional cubist-style canvases. Whilst I appreciated the political statement of the artwork – though what it was escaped me – I still preferred my insipid landscapes, as Luca had called them that fateful night at the gallery.

"Serpentine Hall has three floors. We are standing on the first floor of the east wing. All the bedrooms are on the first floor, divided between the west and east wing."

"How efficient," I murmured, recalling Flora's earlier description of Helen. Whilst I admired her efficiency, what was hiding behind Helen's business-like façade? Her face was taut, as if someone had gathered the skin at the back of her neck with a clothes peg.

"The ground floor below us houses the dining room, ballroom, drawing room, morning room, study, conservatory, library, serving room, and an art studio. Below that, you'll find the wine cellar, larder, billiard room, coal room, and kitchen."

Ruby pointed at my door. "Why does Fina's door have a

brown canvas on it? My door has an indigo canvas."

Miss Poole arched an eyebrow. "Sir Montague insisted that each bedroom have a colour attached to it, and each colour has a specific painting pigment name. Yours, as you said, is Indigo."

"And mine is brown?" I asked.

"Yours is Burnt Umber," she corrected.

Ruby held her hand to her mouth, suppressing a giggle.

"And your friend, Mr Hayford, is staying in the Magenta room," said Miss Poole.

I forced down a grimace. Of course my room was drab Burnt Umber. But I ignored the slight and pushed on. "You said all the bedrooms are on this floor. Does that include yours and Mr Benbow's?"

She pushed back the curl of hair covering her eye. "Yes, Sir Montague is very forward in his thinking. My room is next to yours, Miss Aubrey-Havelock."

I squinted at her door. "What colour is that? Green?"

"Viridian," said Ruby, who loved dabbling in dyes for her clothing designs.

"Well spotted, Miss Dove," said Miss Poole. "Let me show you the rest of the house." Her stiff skirt seemed to move of its own accord as we passed the Turner's Yellow room next to mine and then the Burgundy bedroom beyond.

At the staircase landing, Miss Poole said, "To our right is the long gallery, overlooking the sea and filled with Sir Montague's favourite artwork. If you continue forward, you'll reach the west wing."

She slid her hand down a wide wood-carved bannister adorned with grinning gargoyles that, whilst playful enough in the daytime, would unleash the horrors should I bump into them at night.

I looked up at the approaching sound of footsteps. "Oh, pardon me," I said, moving to one side.

The man ascending the stairs had a heavy, deliberate step. He raised his mop of dark hair, one errant wisp playing across his forehead. A crooked nose, one that had been broken and not set properly, peeked out from below his heavy brow.

"Niall Rafferty," he said gruffly, holding out his hand to Ruby. Beyond his unusual appearance, Niall had set himself apart by greeting Ruby first – something that rarely happened when we were together. Then he made even more of an impression by not acknowledging my presence at all.

"Mr Rafferty is our resident psychotherapist," said Miss Poole, as if he were an eccentric uncle living in the attic. "And this is Miss Fina Aubrey-Havelock and Miss Ruby Dove."

"Flora has spoken your praises, Mr Rafferty," said Ruby. "She says your new techniques will be revolutionary."

"Well, Miss Dove," he said in a light Dublin accent, "I save the word 'revolutionary' for special political occasions, but I appreciate the kind words. Now, if you'll excuse me." With only a glance at me, he continued up the stairs.

I blurted, "It's a pleasure to meet you as well."

He looked back, a tiny smile playing across his lips. "I won't be joining you for lunch, Miss Poole," he called as he moved up the stairs.

When he'd disappeared from sight, I asked, "Is he always so rude?"

Miss Poole brushed her throat. "I've only just met him, but he can be rather abrupt."

"Maybe he's preoccupied with a fiendishly complicated psychotherapy case," Ruby said as we entered the grand hall downstairs.

Miss Poole walked ahead, but Ruby shortened her step enough to remain out of earshot.

She whispered, "Curious, isn't it? Within ten minutes of meeting Miss Poole, she's already lied to us."

7

"Ah! Our intrepid guests arrive," boomed Sir Montague, stretching his arms wide. A man loyal to his dressing routine, he wore a smoking jacket and cravat, just as he had at the gallery opening. His blue eyes twinkled with a soupçon of mischief.

He bowed in my direction. "I pray our mermaid has also recovered."

I returned his bow with a ridiculous involuntary curtsey. "Apologies for creating such a scene. I'm much better now, thanks to Miss Poole's assistance."

Not one to let a compliment go unnoticed, Sir Montague rhapsodised in a poetic cadence, "Miss Poole is the most spectacular secretary and housekeeper a man ever had."

Though Helen's hair shaded her eye, the colour rose in her pale cheeks.

"And her voice is like honey," he continued.

Miss Poole quickly changed the subject. "Ruby and Fina, shall we continue the tour after lunch?"

"You see? She cannot help herself. We must follow the plan!" Sir Montague clapped his hands. "'A thing of beauty is a joy forever: its loveliness increases; it will never pass into nothingness ..."' He rumbled on, reciting the entire poem by Keats.

"He ought to go on the stage if this painter business fails," whispered Pixley. Like Sir Montague, Pixley wore a dark-indigo smoking jacket and a white gossamer cravat. Any other person might take offence at the similarity in their unique dress, but not Sir Montague. He was secure in his own originality, and would even wear a potato sack with flair.

"I see our journalist friend has joined us." Sir Montague motioned towards Pixley. "And whilst I approve of your clothing choices, I warn you, young man, I will not tolerate any scurrilous stories written about myself or my guests."

"Aye, aye, Sir Montague." Pixley saluted him. "Message received."

A cuckoo clock chimed in the corner. A bird shot out, wearing a tiny purple wig and a pink knitted jumper. Most unusual. But it was a house of an artist, I reminded myself. One must expect the unexpected.

Sir Montague rubbed his hands together. "Now, we shall adjourn for a delectable lunch, and then our young artists will commence with their masterpieces."

Our gathering trundled after Sir Montague towards the dining room. I peeked through the open doors, noting a study and a narrow serving room to my right, and a studio flooded with light, easels, and canvases to my left.

In the serving room, a placid Mr Benbow was easing a gleaming soup tureen onto a tray laden with bowls, plates, and a cascade of silver spoons. He eyed us and plodded towards the door.

He winked and nodded at me, so I slowed my progress. "Would you like help with that tray, Mr Benbow?"

I must have overdone my attempt at a casual tone as Ruby

and Pixley both looked over. But the thought of food must have drawn them onwards to the dining room.

Peering around the corner, Mr Benbow whispered, "Come in here for a moment, miss."

Once we moved out of earshot, his affable, creased face suddenly smoothed. He worked his jaw side to side, like a cow savouring its well-chewed meal. "Don't know how to tell you this, but what happened at the jetty just now weren't an accident. No, miss. You were pushed like a sheep blocking a motorcar."

"You mean Mr Gatti?" I asked. "But why?"

He scratched his head with a white hand covered in spiky black hair. "Can't rightly say, miss. But you watch that one. He's cleverer than a bag of ferrets."

"What do you mean?"

"I help out with Sir Montague's paintings and such when I'm in London. Now, I'm not a quick wit like those posh Londoners, and I didn't take any university degrees like you and your friends, but I do have a good memory." He tapped his head. "And I can't make head nor tail of it, but that Mr Gatti is trouble. Mark my words. And watch the others too, miss."

"Why are you telling me all this?"

"Peculiar things have been happening here, miss. And your swim in the sea was one example. Helen told me all about the happenings and I believe her, even if we don't always see eye to eye." He gave a gentle snort. "More like she has an eye on Sir Montague – designs on him, that is."

Though I was hungry for more gossip, our conversation broke off at a pattering noise like a tiny horse galloping. A flash of orange hurtled past us into the dining room, followed by a shattering of glass and a shriek. We hurried towards the dining room.

"Tangerine!" Flora stood at one end of the dining room overlooking the frothy sea, stroking an orange kitten in her arms. Shards of glass glinted around her ballet-slippered feet. "I'm so sorry, Helen!" she said. "What's gotten into Reen today?"

Helen's split-second frown arched into a placating smile. "No trouble at all, Miss Scott. I'll fetch a dustpan." She turned on her heel and hurried from the room.

Tangerine leapt from Flora's arms and dashed after Helen. I tried and failed to stroke the cat as she shot past me.

"Enough with the cats. I'm famished!" Daphne glided into the room wearing a gold satin tea gown, a white fur draped about her. Though the gold satin leaned towards a gala evening in London, the tea-dress cut saved her from being overdressed. As if Daphne could ever be such a thing.

Ruby's left eyebrow rose as Daphne took a seat at the head of the table. Flapping her serviette open, Daphne said, "I detect a gleam in your eye, Ruby. Rest assured, I'm simply rejecting a fatuous tradition of ordering everyone around the table in a silly game of rank. Head of the table is a chair, not a status."

Sir Montague strode in and sat at the opposite end of the table, grumbling under his breath and avoiding Daphne's eye. He also shook his serviette with a crack.

"Please, everyone, sit. John will be serving."

Luca slipped into the chair to my right. "Which room are you in, Fina?" he asked as if we'd just met.

Wary of his intentions, I shrunk back in my chair.

"Apologies." He picked up his soup spoon and put it down again. "That was impertinent. But it's a fantastic idea to name rooms after paint pigments. Have you noticed how they fit our personalities? Daphne is in Turner's Yellow and Flora is in Azure."

"Did you call my name?" asked Flora.

Luca jiggled his leg. "I was just saying how the room colours match our personalities."

Ruby leaned over. "I believe your Azure means you like to innovate, Flora. Perfect for your artistic creations."

"Huh." Flora's tongue stretched the inside of her cheek. "I hadn't paid attention to the personality part, like you said, Luca. Blue isn't my favourite colour, so I assumed it was random. But what Ruby says is true – I do love an experiment!"

"Now my mind is awash with new ideas for the gallery." Luca withdrew a small notebook from his pocket and drummed his fingers on it. "Helen just gave me this to jot down ideas."

His childlike enthusiasm lowered my guard, but I still felt churlish and vaguely obstinate. "I'm in the Burnt Umber room," I said flatly.

From across the table, Pixley winked at me. "Don't be too cross. Did you notice the Zinc White room? Whoever is staying there must have no personality at all. Whereas Burnt Umber evokes hidden depths."

"An excellent effort, Pix," I said sourly. "In my mind, all it evokes is mud."

Wisely giving up on his quest to convince me otherwise, Pixley lifted his chin at Luca. "Yours is Vermilion."

"I find it a rather overexcited colour." As if proving his point, he said this in almost a whisper.

"Oh, come now, Mr Gatti." Pixley polished his spectacles.

"Everyone calls me Luca."

"Well, as I was saying, Luca, you seem like an ambitious chap. After all, running a successful gallery in London must be deuced difficult. I couldn't muster the focus needed to accomplish such a feat. No, I'm more omnivorous in my tastes – hence my Magenta room."

Unable or unwilling to speak, Luca shifted his eyes from side to side.

Pixley motioned towards Helen Poole as she was carrying

away the dustpan. "Miss Poole, who's in the charmingly vapid 'Zinc White' room?"

She pushed back the curl of hair from her face. "Mr Charles Vane is in that room. He should arrive with Gwendolyn Brice shortly."

"Who is this Mr Charles Vane, Sir Montague?" asked Pixley in a burst of journalistic impulsivity.

Sir Montague wiped his lips with his napkin. "I see you cannot help yourself, young man. A journalist sniffing out a story." He gave an indulgent snort. "Well, I'm afraid you'll have to ask Mr Vane yourself. He's Gwendolyn's judge, and I know as much – or as little – as you."

Daphne twisted the stem of her glass. "Talking of the contest, what are the rules this weekend, Sir Montague? Not that I'm bound to follow them."

My focus shifted to slurping the brown Windsor soup, an action that caused extreme facial spasms. I hoped the contortions would go unnoticed.

No such luck, of course. Holding up her napkin as a shield, Ruby whispered, "You also think the soup tastes like boiled socks, don't you?"

"Ra-ther," I said. "My gastric juices anxiously await the next course. After all, who has ever had a truly tasty bowl of Windsor soup?"

As if to contradict me, Sir Montague lifted the soup bowl to his mouth, tilted it backwards, and sucked down the lot. He smacked his lips and suppressed a belch. "You've outdone yourself again, Helen."

A rash-like redness spread across her pink face.

Sir Montague pushed on, turning to Daphne. "Now, to answer your question about our competition, the rules are the following."

His forefinger sprung up. "First, judges shall not interrupt the painters during the sittings."

Another finger. "Second, judges may not view the portraits until they are complete. Third, the contest shall commence as soon as Miss Brice arrives. That is, Miss Scott and Miss Brice shall have thirty-six hours to craft their masterpieces."

Flora shifted in her seat. "Thirty-six hours? When will we sleep? I may look like I run on electricity, but I must have my shut-eye. I'm not like Luca, who can run for days on end."

Sir Montague trained his watery eyes on Flora. "In my young day, a painter would stay up for days to complete a portrait."

Flora sighed and stabbed her fork at a boiled carrot, more of a sickly parsnip-yellow than bright orange.

I lifted a limp, quivering courgette on my fork. It tasted exactly like the smell of rotting fish, though the poor vegetable had never even enjoyed the freedom of the open sea. Resisting a gagging impulse, I gulped it down whole.

Ruby's fork zigzagged around her plate, rearranging her food into neat piles in a clear attempt to make them disappear. Pixley's strategy was to shovel piles of flaccid courgettes into his mouth as fast as possible. Luca had given up altogether and was tapping his forefinger on the table, though I doubted he ever ate much, given his rail-thin physique. Flora had pushed her plate towards the empty seat next to her, as if it belonged to this wraithlike guest. And Daphne had simply requested another glass of wine, forgoing any pretence of lunch.

I held out hope for the pudding. If there was any pudding.

"Fourth," Sir Montague rumbled on, "no monkey business. Is that understood?" He levelled his fork at each of us, pausing when he came to Daphne.

Daphne chuckled. "Don't point your prongs at me. I'm the picture of a rule follower."

At that, we all broke out in a welcome round of laughter.

Sir Montague quelled our amusement with another jab of his utensil. "I will not abide any pranks, shenanigans, or other attempts to sabotage a painter or the contest."

A cough from the doorway interrupted him. "Pardon me, sir, but Miss Brice and Mr Vane have arrived. Shall I show them into the dining room?"

"By all means, John. By all means." He rubbed his hands together. "Then we will begin."

Flora rocketed from her seat. "I've finished my meal. May I be excused, Sir Montague?" She fluttered her eyelashes like a child seeking a reprieve from adult company.

"Where are you rushing off to?" asked Daphne. "Aren't you curious about our mysterious guest?"

Without a word, Sir Montague closed and opened his eyes, motioning a dampening hand at Flora.

Flora was not one to be restricted in her movements, whether in her clothes or being excused from the table. But Sir Montague apparently held sway over her. She sat again, though this time she sat cross-legged in a minor act of defiance.

Helen had placed a generous helping of spotted dick in front of me. I took my first bite, all my senses concentrating on the lovely, gooey, sticky mess.

Dreadful. Simply dreadful. Those were words I'd never used for a pudding before. Dull or passable, yes, but never dreadful. Helen had not only poured the entire sugar contents of the larder into her mixing bowl but had also added rancid suet for good measure. I edged the bowl away, my five senses gradually returning to my surroundings.

Even Pixley had pushed away his bowl. Fortunately for all of us, what sounded like a herd of baby elephants echoed from the hallway. It had to be Miss Brice given the heavy yet rapid footsteps, a pair of feet I'd not soon forget after our contretemps at the Finch Gallery.

Gwendolyn Brice marched in, wearing a black silk dress tied at the waist with a crimson sash, matching the red tip of her white nose. Her frizzy, middle-parted bob held water droplets from the sea voyage to Cutmere Perch. She fingered the large cameo choker necklace threatening to strangle her thin neck, but her strong, ropy cords of muscle flexed and pulsed, fighting back against the cameo of a Victorian woman.

Her eyes scanned our party, and then, squinting in a sudden shaft of sunlight from the window, she stared at me with those tiny mole-like eyes.

Though Gwendolyn's stare was unnerving, it was nothing compared to the figure looming behind her. The quick intake of breath near me signalled I wasn't the only one surprised by our mysterious guest.

8

I gripped Ruby's arm, goggling at the man propping up the door frame. A wisp of cigarette smoke brushed his temple in its lazy ascent to the ceiling.

Ruby dug her fingernails into my hand, though I barely noticed the painful jabbing.

Dumbfounded. That's what I was. Mr Vane must be related to Ruby's old flame, Ian Clavering. The cut of the jaw, the sticking-out ears, and the quick, wicked grin clearly belonged to the Claverings from Barbados.

Like Ian, Mr Vane was a careful dresser; his light-grey worsted suit hung loosely on his slender frame, and a scarlet handkerchief peeked out of his breast pocket, matching the just-visible silk lining of his jacket.

In a rare parody of a goldfish, Ruby opened and closed her mouth, her words trapped in her throat. Since I'd known her, Ruby's minor flirtations had never blossomed into even minor romances. The man from Barbados had truly stolen her heart. Ian Clavering, theatre producer and ostensible spy for various Caribbean causes, had the knack of popping up unannounced and then toddling off. He'd always pack Ruby's heart in his travelling case, but leave the woman behind.

Helen Poole's eyebrows knitted together, looking from Charles to Ruby. "Everyone has met Miss Brice, but we have another judge with us this weekend. A Mr Charles Vane, with Ledburn and Lamport, a molasses company. Pardon, a sugar company." She turned towards him. "Is that correct, Mr Vane?"

Mr Vane beamed. "Quite right. For my sins, I'm afraid." He scanned the crowd with a blank stare. But his next movement raised the hair on my arms. His eyebrows wiggled as he glanced at Ruby – just like Ian Clavering. Unlike Ian, however, the Y-shaped vein on his forehead pulsed even as the rest of his face remained impassive.

Ruby had regained control of herself and was gazing at a sunflower painting opposite her. She and Mr Vane were now locked in an absurd game of non-recognition. Whilst I couldn't be certain Mr Vane had seen Ruby before, his studied avoidance suggested he must know something about her.

Finally ending the stand-off, Ruby strode forward with an outstretched hand. "A pleasure to meet you, Mr Vane. I'm Ruby Betto Dove. Believe it or not, I've heard your name before – though it couldn't have been you."

"Why ever not, dear lady? Though Charles and Vane are common, I've met no one with my name before." His voice held the same precise, clipped intonation as Ian's, but it was high-pitched compared to Ian's pleasant tenor. And unlike Ian, Charles Vane had a smile in his voice: when he bared his teeth, it rose another octave.

Ruby ran her tongue along her top lip, hesitating. "My grandmother in St Kitts loved to tell me stories. Mostly stories about history, lessons I'd never learn at school."

No one moved. Though the words were commonplace, the

atmosphere crackled. Every face was frozen as if Charles and Ruby were the only two people allowed to speak.

Charles cocked his head at an angle. Every movement of his facial muscles was deliberate, sharp, and mechanical. Except the eyebrow wiggling, of course. "My grandmother also told me such stories, Miss Dove. But I'm unfamiliar with any tales of Charles Vane."

"He was a pirate in the sixteen hundreds, famous for his daring feats against the British empire. Though I much prefer other pirates, such as Henri Caesar, Diego Grillo, or Hendrick Quintor."

Charles ignored Ruby's list. "It is a most fascinating history, but I can claim no lineage to that particular Mr Vane. I'm simply plain Charles Vane." He paused. "Though I have met plenty of people pretending to be someone else."

A loud smashing of glass rescued Ruby from this stand-off. Helen Poole's large cut-glass bowl of spotted dick had slipped from her hands, creating a gloopy yellow mess on the floor.

Helen scooped the custard with her hands.

"No, Helen—" Mr Benbow dashed towards her.

But Mr Benbow's words came too late. In a pinching motion, Helen had grasped a glass shard with two fingers, but the ghastly lumpy mixture hid another piece of glass. Helen shot up, screeching as the custard oozed down her arm, turning from yellow to brown.

Charles draped his scarlet handkerchief from his pocket around Helen's arm, creating an impromptu tourniquet. "It will hold for a moment," he said, "but we need something else to tie around her arm. Quickly!"

A thud came from the window.

Pixley rushed behind the table. "Flora has fainted dead away."

Daphne fled into the hallway. "We need a doctor!"

"Where is she going?" Sir Montague asked as he stripped off his smoking jacket, probably to create another tourniquet. We all ran about, offering larger and more ridiculous items of clothing to pack around Helen's arm, or to put underneath Flora on the floor.

"I believe she's fetching Mr Rafferty," wheezed Mr Benbow. "Perhaps he has medical training."

The blood streamed down Helen's arm.

Gwendolyn scrabbled in her bag, yanking out a black scarf that she wrapped around Charles's handkerchief.

"It will be all right, Helen." Luca held a firm hand on her shoulder. "Just look at me. Focus on me."

A breathless Daphne returned with Niall Rafferty in tow, his customary frown only deepening at the chaotic scene meeting his eyes.

"Let me get Helen to the kitchen." Niall's eyes darted around the room. "Daphne said Flora had fainted. Where is she?"

"Over here," said Pixley. I hoisted myself over the table, nearly lying flat in an effort to see over it. He was cradling Flora's head.

"A brandy might help," called Pixley.

Niall leaned over the table as well, brushing against my arm. Then he pointed at me. "You. Elevate her feet. And you, Luca, fetch her a brandy."

Niall then turned on his heel and strode from the room, piloting Helen as he went. Luca scurried behind, presumably in search of brandy.

I lowered myself onto my knees, stuffing Flora's shawl under her slippered feet. Before disappearing behind the table, I noticed Sir Montague raking his hand over his face.

It might have been my fancy, but there was a quaver in his

sonorous baritone. "This will never do," he sighed. "It's a most inauspicious beginning to our weekend. But I will allow no one to interfere with my young artists."

9

Momentary surges of sunlight cast long shadows in the darkened corridor leading to the west wing bedrooms. A cloud passed over, plunging Gwendolyn and me into a twilight state and setting the paintings aglow along the wall. Even Gwendolyn's yellowing teeth gleamed in the half-light.

She jerked her head to the left. "Come with me."

I stood irresolute, unable to shake the scene we'd left behind in the dining room. Flora still lay unconscious on the sofa, though Helen now had a proper bandage after Niall and John's quick work in the kitchen.

Gwendolyn peered at me. "Is something the matter? It's as dark as a cow's stomach in here, but my room has plenty of natural light."

I ran my fingers through my fringe. "It's not that. It's just, how can you begin painting if Flora is still unconscious? Isn't it against the rules?"

"Whilst you were downstairs in the kitchen, Flora came to and began burbling about beginning as soon as possible. Your friends tried to persuade her to rest, but she was most adamant."

She paused. "Sir Montague agreed with her, though reluctantly."

Flora's voice came up behind us. "He did at that. I insisted."

Ruby and Flora stood on the landing. Ruby's face stood in the shadows, making it look older and tired. Flora's eyes sparkled, however, with tiny bonfires lit in each pupil.

"Flora relishes a challenge," said Ruby. The half-smile on Ruby's face suggested this quality ought to be feared and admired. Though the smile could be due to her encounter with her boyfriend's doppelgänger.

Flora's eyes narrowed. "And may the best woman win."

Gwendolyn sniffed. "I'd prefer to say, 'May the best painter win'."

Stretching her arms wide and high, Flora said, "I'm the complete package, as we say in New York. I can be a woman and a painter at the same time."

"Ladies!" said Luca, his voice rising. He had padded up the stairs like a cat, completely unnoticed until he spoke with fervour.

A breathless Daphne came up behind him. "Luca Gatti, don't you 'lady' Flora and Gwendolyn. They certainly don't need anyone else telling them what they ought to do."

Gwendolyn whispered to me, "That Daphne boils like pea soup. Never stops talking."

Daphne's head jerked towards Gwendolyn. "Pardon. What did you say?"

Gwendolyn shook her head.

Daphne sauntered towards her with her hips leading, like a vamp in a film. All she was missing was a long cigarette holder.

She moved less than an inch away from Gwendolyn's nose. "If you 'ave something to say about me, say it to my face." Daphne's Sheffield accent had crept in, complete with dropped *h*'s.

Gwendolyn crossed her arms. Instead of speaking to Daphne, she looked at me. "Mae hi'n siarad fel melin bupur."

"What did she say?" Flora licked her lips. This American loved a fight.

"I know that Welsh saying." Luca's eyes twinkled. "Gwendolyn said you talk like a pepper mill, Daphne. It means you talk non-stop."

Ruby grasped Daphne's shoulder before she could move any closer to Gwendolyn. "Deep breaths, Daphne. We are all under a lot of strain. Why don't you go paint in your room? Didn't Niall prescribe painting for you?"

Like a child distracted from crying with the bribe of a biscuit, Daphne beamed at Ruby. "Quite right. He says I ought to work out all my inner struggles over my childhood through painting red and black paintings. Helps release anger, apparently."

A mollified Daphne meant Gwendolyn and I could make our escape. Gwendolyn trundled a few steps ahead of me, weaving to the left, past Luca's Vermilion room and Charles Vane's Zinc White. We turned right, down the hallway past Chrome Orange, Cobalt, and finally to the Perylene Black at the end of the corridor, overlooking the rear of Serpentine Hall and the jagged grey-green rocks.

She opened the Perylene Black door. I'd never seen the colour before, but it was more than simple black: it was luminescent, like a black opal.

"Enter," she said.

In a wild flight of fancy, I pictured Gwendolyn locking me in and cackling maniacally.

I shook myself from this nightmare, more curious than afraid of Gwendolyn's eccentric personality, not to mention the contents of her room. A room has a lot to say about its owner.

To my right stood a floor-to-ceiling bank of windows overlooking the cliffs. The clouds had cleared and the horizon was empty of passing boats. The green sea churned and bubbled, washing over the rocks below like a foamy milk concoction. Like that delicious frothy cocktail I'd had in a new so-called "milk bar" in London.

Near the rocks, the glassed-in windows of the conservatory sat below us and a jagged pathway wound along the scrabbly clifftop.

I drew back from the window's light, momentarily blinded as my eyes adjusted to the gloom of the black walls. This wasn't a cheerful room – it was as austere and severe as its inhabitant.

Responding to my unspoken thoughts, Gwendolyn said, "I prefer natural light. So let's begin whilst there's still sunlight, as weak as it is."

Her easel stood ready in one corner, opposite a hard wooden chair near the window.

"Sit down," she said.

I sighed, resigning myself to the rigid chair. At least it was low to the floor, so my legs wouldn't dangle. As I smoothed my skirt to sit down, I pointed to a plump scatter cushion on her four-poster bed. "May I sit on that cushion? The chair looks a trifle abrasive."

With a paintbrush between her teeth, Gwendolyn wrinkled her nose. Then she squeezed a fat red snake of paint onto a clean palette.

So I sat on the hard chair with my arms rigid, as if I were waiting outside the headmistress's office. I'd been called into the headmistress's only once, thanks to a budding extortionist named Tommy Drinkwater. He'd threatened to tell our teacher I cheated in our history exam – an utterly baseless accusation, I assure you – unless I supplied him the answers. When the teacher discovered this racket, Tommy said I was the ringleader.

Last I'd heard, grown-up Tommy had graduated to fleecing wealthy old ladies.

"Relax, Fina. You look like a dog sitting on a fence." Gwendolyn held up her paintbrush, a red paint glob dangling from it. "After all, I'm not going to bite."

She flipped her paintbrush into the air, spattering the red paint against the black wall, then flashed her yellowing teeth again, directly contradicting this statement.

"I'll do my best."

My words wouldn't have convinced even the most gullible soul. But I was too preoccupied with my sore backside and the wafting metallic odour of oil paint filling the room.

"How can you stand the oil paint odour, especially in your bedroom?"

Gwendolyn wriggled her nose and inhaled. "I quite like it."

No wonder Van Gogh went mad, I thought, recalling Gwendolyn's dramatic scene in the gallery. The oil paint fumes had probably infected his brain – and hers, too.

"I'm terribly sorry, but the odour is making me woozy. May I open a window?"

"I suppose – I'm just painting a bit before I start your sketch. Helps set the right mood."

Before she changed her mind, I'd unlatched the paned windows and leaned out, breathing in the light salt gusts. The sea had calmed, so I enjoyed the expansive freedom before returning to the cloistered room.

Rustling leaves shifted my eyes from the horizon to the scrubby garden right below the window.

"Psst ... Red! Down here!"

10

From the garden below, Pixley squinted up at me.

"Psst ... Rapunzel, Rapunzel, let down your hair!"

I shook my short locks, parodying the kidnapped heroine after her unfortunate encounter with the scissors. "Sir Hayford, please rescue me! We haven't even begun Gwendolyn's painting and I'm already itching to leave."

A glance over my shoulder at Gwendolyn's busy paintbrush confirmed she hadn't heard me. Or was too engrossed to care.

"Dashed peculiar group of people altogether," said Pixley. "Even I find them exhausting. And why the devil has Ian Clavering's twin popped up this weekend, of all weekends? Deuced odd coincidence."

"Did you speak to Mr Vane?"

"I squeezed in a few words before we were interrupted. Charles said he was on a job and had heard of Ian Clavering, but Sir Montague barged in, bellowing in his foghorn voice that Charles ought to steer clear of me."

"Why?" I asked, humouring him.

"Can you believe it? He doesn't trust my snooping tendencies."

"Well, riddle me this, professional snoop: a dead ringer for Ian wangles an invitation to a remote island where Ruby just happens to be as well? And what is the relationship between sugar and art?"

"Now who's been to the pictures too often?" Pixley winked at me. "Dead ringer, indeed."

I stamped my foot. "It's a common enough phrase."

"Well, I agree it's most peculiar. But never fear, your intrepid journalist will soon suss out the truth." He snapped his fingers. "I know my line – I'll ask Charles about the coal loaders' strike in St Lucia. Remember the newspaper headline? If he's involved with the sugar trade in the Caribbean, he'll be watching those events. Those sugar barons will be trying to save their own precious hides. Ruby must know about it, too. Maybe even you?"

I held a finger to my lips. Speaking about our activities was an unnecessary risk, even if Gwendolyn wasn't listening.

He held his hand to his mouth. "Sorry. It's not like me to be so indiscreet. Mum's the word."

A sudden wave loomed behind Pixley and crashed against the rocks, spraying his jacket.

"I don't like it, Pix. Something is brewing."

Pixley brushed away the spray from his sleeves. "The only thing brewing is a storm. You're always affected by a dramatic atmosphere, and Cornish weather makes you see things that aren't there."

He turned. "Talking of things that are there, someone's coming. Must dash. Toodle-pip and all that."

Luca came into view to the right, trotting along the narrow earthen path. His body bounced up and down as tightly as a coiled spring.

In a quick two-step motion, Daphne struggled to keep pace behind him. Although Daphne loved chattering about the liberation of women, her tight skirt prevented her from keeping up with the man in front. I scolded myself for such catty thoughts.

"Luca!" she hissed. "Wait!"

In a terse dismissal, he held up a hand and stared straight ahead.

Daphne halted on the cliff path, flouncing her hands at her sides. As she stood there, a playful gust of wind lifted her floppy hat and tossed it into the sea. She screeched in frustration, and then, in a quick recovery, she shrugged.

But her dramatic scene had worked. Luca had stopped, waiting for her to catch up.

Like a Pomeranian on a stroll, she trundled towards him with tiny, furious steps.

Once she caught him up, she poked her finger at his chest. "Look here, I can only promise seven. We agreed on ten, but I can only guarantee seven. I've already agreed on six for another."

He ran his hands through his thatched blond hair. "All right. But this is my limit, understand?"

She nodded without another word. I struggled to interpret the look on her face, settling on sadness melting into fear.

"Fina!" rasped Gwendolyn behind me. Really, the woman must be a secret smoker. I hadn't noticed it before, but she rattled and wheezed like my great-uncle Hubert, who'd smoked like a chimney his whole life. I wrinkled my nose, recalling how he'd smelled like one too.

"Be with you in a moment." I scanned the cliff path once more. Luca strode forward with his shoulders back whilst Daphne walked a step behind him, head down. It didn't appear to be a lover's tiff, though with Daphne, you never knew. Flora had said Daphne had voracious appetites – of all sorts.

"I've folded a blanket on your chair," called Gwendolyn. "A

pillow will lift you too high, but a blanket will still give you a cushion."

My mind raced as I sat in the chair, mulling over the meaning of "seven" and "ten". Then a silver-framed photograph on a writing desk near the window caught my eye. It must have belonged to Gwendolyn, as it was the only photograph in the room. Indeed, a stack of paintings against the wardrobe door explained why the walls were bare.

The two sullen children peering out from the photograph wore clothing styles from twenty years ago. I guessed the girl must be Gwendolyn, and perhaps the boy was her brother.

Again, with her uncanny ability to read my mind, Gwendolyn said, "The walls are bare because I cannot abide other people's paintings on the wall when I paint. Too distracting and influencing."

"May I speak normally?" I asked through the corner of my mouth.

"Of course you may. I'm not painting a statue – I'm painting a live human being."

Then she jerked her head towards the photograph on the desk. "You're intrigued by the photograph, aren't you?"

"Now you mention it, yes – if it's not too difficult to talk whilst you paint."

"You're a keen observer, aren't you?" Gwendolyn asked, ignoring my response.

"Well, yes," I replied inanely, a reflex habit when I didn't have time to consider a proper answer.

"It takes a true observer of life to recognise and appreciate another one. That's why I chose you for the portrait."

"You're very kind."

"Kindness has nothing to do with it. Have you ever noticed the eyes of observers? They have an incisive sharpness but a distance too."

I hadn't a clue what she meant, but since her pencil was now flying across the canvas, I judged it best to encourage her. "I'm afraid it's not a skill, nor even a trait. It's a compulsion. Almost like breathing."

"Quite. You chased me at the gallery opening for that reason, didn't you?" She scratched her cheek with the pencil and frowned. "But why did you fly at me like a hellhound after his supper?"

A laugh rumbled deep in my belly. It was all utterly ridiculous. But I didn't want it to ruin the sketch, so I held my breath and spoke in little halting bursts. "You'll never believe it. But I thought you had dynamite. Not a candle."

A dry heaving noise arose. My eyes fixed on the window, hoping to catch sight of this bellowing seal on the rocks.

Then Gwendolyn's head moved into view again, and I realised it wasn't a seal. Instead, she was laughing – clearly a rare activity for her.

"It wasn't so amusing at the time," I said, resisting the urge to cross my arms in disapproval.

Gwendolyn wheezed and rattled. "Your face was such a picture!"

Then she wiped her eyes, regaining her composure. "There. Now it's time to transition."

I brightened, sitting up straight like a dog about to receive a treat. "It's time for a tea break? With chocolate biscuits?"

Gwendolyn set down her pencil and surveyed her canvas. "A break of sorts, I suppose, but certainly not one involving biscuits, chocolate or otherwise."

Her eyes fixed on me.

"It's time for you to disrobe."

11

"Pardon?" I asked, trying to ignore my tightening stomach. "Did you say wardrobe? Shall I fetch you something from the wardrobe?"

Gwendolyn set down her paint palette. "I said, it's time to remove your clothes. Disrobe. Put on your birthday suit, if you prefer."

My hand flew to my neck. I wasn't a prude, but well, dash it, I didn't sign up to be naked! To make matters worse, my face itched with a prickly heat.

"Apologies," I said, "but you never mentioned anything about nakedness." My mind flashed back over Gwendolyn's paintings from a catalogue Flora had shown me. I didn't remember a single nude portrait – unless you counted the cats.

Feeling vindicated, I said, "After all, aren't portraits usually of people wearing clothes?"

Gwendolyn let out a snort-chuckle. "That's true, but it's not how I work. I can only take the true measure of my subject once I see them in the flesh."

Flesh. My skin crawled at the word.

In retaliation, I also crossed my arms. "And I'm doubtful Ruby will agree to be naked, either."

"Unless she's changed, Flora doesn't use my technique. So Miss Dove will remain fully clothed."

Suddenly Gwendolyn's fist banged on a side table, sending her paint tubes rolling onto the floor. Her red-rimmed eyes fixed on me with an icy stare. "It's sabotage. At every turn, it's sabotage, isn't it?" Though she was staring at me, she was speaking to herself.

She lifted her chin, making a pinched gurgling noise. "Yes, that's it. They've done it again."

With my back against the wall, I inched towards the door. *Keep her talking, Fina, keep her talking. She's stark-raving bonkers.*

"Who is 'they'?" I asked in a high-pitched whine.

"Sir Montague, Flora, Luca ... the whole London art world."

"The entire London art world?"

Her fist came down again. "Yes, the entire cursed mob of half-witted, half-sober, vulgar layabouts. A flock of sheep have more taste than those ninnies."

"Well, why don't I try to remedy this minor hiccup, shall I? I'll just toddle off to find a few neutral parties downstairs."

I was within arm's reach of the door. If I could just—

Gwendolyn snorted. "Neutral parties, my foot. This house is filled with spies, I tell you. Mark my words, Fina. Spies."

∼

I SLAMMED Gwendolyn's door and hurtled down the corridor. Along the way, I heard glass clinking in Charles's room, a whooshing, scraping noise of sweeping in Mr Benbow's, and the tap-tap sound of a typewriter in Daphne's room. But even these curiosities failed to halt my progress. I flew down the steps, through the conservatory, and out through the French doors into the frigid night air.

Now free from Gwendolyn's clutches, I needed to think. Pixley was nowhere about, and I didn't fancy interrupting Flora and Ruby. Telling them about Gwendolyn's accusation of sabotage would only make matters worse.

The conservatory's glassed-in structure cast a glow outside, offering enough light to gain my bearings. I stood beside a hedge, ready to hide behind it should someone wander into the conservatory.

Like Miss Garbo, I wanted to be alone.

From somewhere inside, a door slammed shut. Sir Montague strode into the conservatory as if this were the opening to a play on the stage. Crouching down behind the hedge, I concealed myself just as the French doors opened. Sir Montague coughed, and another set of footsteps soon followed behind him onto the terrace.

"Ah, Sir Montague. Right on time," purred Charles.

"There is no right time, my boy, but this will suffice." Sir Montague sighed. "Here, I poured a drink for you."

Glasses clinked.

"Now, about this spot of bother in St Lucia," said Charles. "The prime minister is eager to avoid this spreading. He's particularly concerned about Barbados catching it."

Their voices came closer. I sniffed. Cigarette smoke wafted towards me, so I edged closer to the wall.

"Nonsense – it's not the flu or some cursed disease. It was an isolated incident. And after all, the conditions in St Lucia were abominable."

"No less or more than other Caribbean islands, I assure you. The PM agrees with me," Charles said in a self-satisfied tone.

"Well, what does our illustrious PM suggest we do?"

"Inviting everyone here was a jolly good first step," Charles said. "Now tell me where, or rather on whom, I should focus my eyes and ears."

"I've done as you've asked, my boy. No more and no less."

"You must have an inkling. That Daphne woman is a regular Bolshie if you ask me. She also has the money."

Sir Montague snorted. "Daphne's perfectly harmless. No, I don't believe it's her."

"Well? Who, then?"

"I simply cannot imagine."

Sir Montague paused. "Did you hear that?"

"No. What was it? I cannot hear anything over those tiresome waves."

"Ah, yes. You're most unaccustomed to living by the sea – or at least waves of this sort. I heard a rustling noise."

Charles chuckled. "Someone must be hiding in a rosebush."

"Don't laugh, my boy. You know very well it's possible. Even probable."

Footsteps approached, but their direction was unclear.

Then the French doors banged shut.

Letting out a whoosh of air, my belly expanded and relaxed.

There were those footsteps again, heavy and deliberate. Not like Charles's light and nimble step. Perhaps it was Sir Montague investigating the noise he'd heard.

Flattening myself against the wall, I pushed up the hedge so it would cover my head. All I received for my pains was a sharp prick from an exposed branch.

I bit my lip, repressing a yelp. Blasted hedges. What useless garden accoutrements – better to let gardens run wild like they do in nature.

My mind raced, searching for an excuse should someone spot me. Yes, that's it: I was taking in the sea air. But why was I behind a hedge? Well, I spotted a hedgehog, and I did adore them, even though Ruby was simply terrified of the beasties. No, that wouldn't do. Surely hedgehogs wouldn't live on the island. No one would believe my story for a moment.

The same heavy footsteps interrupted my wandering thoughts. They were much closer this time.

"Hullo. Fancy meeting you here."

12

That Dublin accent was unmistakable.

Rude Niall. Or, more properly, rude Dr Rafferty.

He stepped into the tepid light from the conservatory. "Lovely night for a stroll," he said with a heaping of irony.

An icy gust of wind blew my hair sideways. "Well, I prefer my walks to be invigorating." Even to myself, I sounded like a retired colonel praising the health benefits of a twenty-mile stroll.

"You've certainly got your wish. It's Fina, right?"

"Miss Aubrey-Havelock, yes."

"Ah. Well, Miss Aubrey-Havelock, I don't see how you'll make much progress strolling if you're stuck behind a hedge. Or is this part of a new-fangled exercise craze?"

"If you must know, I was petting Tangerine."

"Tangerine? You mean Miss Scott's cat? That is peculiar now."

"What's peculiar? That Miss Scott has a cat or that I enjoy petting him?"

His lips twitched to the side. "I've just come from a chat with

Miss Scott and your friend Ruby – Miss Dove, that is – and little Tangerine was purring on Miss Scott's lap."

Deciding a diversion was in order, I shot back, "Are you well acquainted with Miss Scott?"

Niall rocked back on his heels. "You know, Miss Aubrey-Havelock, you've caused quite a stir at Serpentine Hall."

"Have I? I cannot see how. I'm most forgettable."

"Hmm, I wonder now." He paused.

"What are you grinning at? It's a most tiresome habit, you know."

"I'm afraid it's an occupational habit, you know."

"To grin at your patients whilst they tell you their deepest secrets and desires?"

"Well, that's just it. I can't do so whilst they're talking, so it all surfaces during my non-patient hours, as it were."

"I'm sure Dr Freud would have thoughts about that."

"Touché. But returning to my earlier point: I spotted you fleeing Gwendolyn's room. The question is, why? I'll admit she's a bit, well, intimidating, but someone who strolls along a clifftop path in the dark must be made of sterner stuff."

The moon had risen, giving Niall's mop of black hair a silvery glow. I considered Charles and Sir Montague's conversation. Clearly, they were searching for a spy or agitator. Niall certainly was sharp enough, and a psychotherapist would be brilliant cover for a spy – you might even gather information from your patients.

"Miss Aubrey-Havelock?"

Niall was staring at me in a most disconcerting manner and I realised I'd become lost in my thoughts again. "Sorry. I was ruminating on Gwendolyn's problem."

"What problem?"

"She wanted me naked," I blurted, much louder than I intended.

He coughed, a cough that crescendoed into a boisterous laugh.

"It's not amusing," I huffed.

"Excuse me, but it is." He held up a hand, unable to catch his breath.

"Who's out there?"

Pixley's stocky figure trotted towards us. "Hi, what's all this?" He rubbed his upper arms. "It's positively arctic out here. Is this a new health treatment? Recommended by the good doctor for stimulating the old grey cells?"

Niall turned, wiping his eye with a finger. "Ah, it's yourself, Mr Hayford. Miss Aubrey-Havelock was amusing me with her stories."

"Was she now?" Pixley lifted an eyebrow. "It wouldn't have to do with posing in the raw, shall we say?"

Pixley dissolved into a spasm of giggles.

"I still can't believe serious-knickers Gwendolyn asked you to pose in the nip," said Niall, cracking yet another smile.

Soon, both Pixley and Niall were doubled over in peals of laughter.

I crossed my arms. "Yes, that's right. Go on, have a laugh at my expense."

Ruby and Flora hurried out through the French doors, joining the growing crowd. "Feens! There you are!" Her voice was already rising with amusement. "We heard—"

I held up a hand. "Yes, you heard I refused to disrobe for Gwendolyn's bally painting." I put my hands on my hips. "A girl does have her dignity."

"Absolutely," Flora put in, biting her upper lip with her bottom teeth.

"Quite right, Feens." Ruby surrendered to a belly laugh. Flora joined in, in tiny breathy squeals like a pig thrilled by the sight of the slop bucket.

Just when I couldn't bear the laughter any longer, my momentary guardian angel stepped out from the conservatory.

"Silence!" boomed Sir Montague.

~

Everyone huddled in the warm conservatory, still recovering from the side-splitting diaphragm exercises I'd provided them with on the terrace.

I tried to find the silver lining; at least my minor mishap had brought welcome levity to a day full of accidents, large and small. After all, I was used to being a source of amusement. And though my ego was bruised, my dignity was still intact.

Sir Montague spread his fingers in a crablike pinching motion around the room, silencing any tittering.

"Now," he said, "I understand we've had a bit of a kerfuffle over the contest. I've assured Gwendolyn we shall continue and will find a solution to her 'little wrinkle', as it were."

"What wrinkle, darlings?" Daphne floated into the room in a shimmering silver gown and feather-covered slippers.

"Fina won't pose for me," sniffed Gwendolyn.

"Steady on, Miss Brice. That's not entirely true, is it?" Pixley said, his face still streaked with tears of laughter. Pix might have a wheeze at my expense occasionally, but he was a loyal friend.

Sir Montague pressed down his hand in a calming motion. "As soon as I learned of Miss Brice's dilemma, I asked Flora to halt her progress."

"It's a shame," sighed Flora. "I was making such progress, wasn't I, Ruby?"

"Agreed," said Ruby. "Though I'd have the same reaction as Fina if you'd asked me to disrobe." Then she smoothed her hair. "Which is why I have an idea."

Niall held up a finger. "Let me guess, Miss Dove. You're going to ask Daphne here, aren't you?"

I enjoyed the rare look of surprise on Ruby's face.

Ruby goggled. "I-I-I, yes, how did you know?"

Niall shrugged.

Daphne lifted her chin. "Well, go on. What were you going to ask me?"

"Perhaps you would be, ah, willing to pose nude for Gwendolyn? Though you're much taller than Fina, you have the same body type." Ruby added, as if a justification were needed, "I notice these things since I design clothes."

"Darling Ruby, you are absolutely marvellous." Daphne primped her hair and gave Gwendolyn a kiss from across the room. "I'll do it, Gwendolyn!"

Pixley whispered, "She's quite the exhibitionist."

He was undoubtedly right, but her proclivities swung in my favour. Soon my embarrassment would be over.

Gwendolyn rubbed her eyes and replaced her spectacles slowly, as if perching them on her nose signalled a grudging agreement.

"I suppose it will have to suffice," she said through pursed lips. "Though I do find it all disruptive. Most disruptive indeed."

She turned to Sir Montague, wagging her finger at his towering figure. "But listen carefully: this isn't the end of it. Someone plans to sabotage this contest. To sabotage me."

13

As we all streamed out of the conservatory, Helen emerged from downstairs wielding a ladle like a magic wand. Even without the sight of her arm in a makeshift sling, I mused it would take more than magic to improve Helen's cooking.

She pointed the ladle at me. "Did I miss this evening's entertainment?"

"How is your arm?" I asked.

Her ladle drooped, mirroring her deepening frown. "I simply cannot manage it. It's quite frustrating. Every dish is burnt because I couldn't move quickly with this cursed arm."

Pixley stepped forward, holding one hand over his round stomach and one behind his back. "I'm sure we're at your service, Miss Poole." He looked at Ruby and me. "Aren't we?"

Poor Helen. She was a dreadful cook, but her inability to complete a task was clearly irksome to her. Then I brightened, thinking that our cooking couldn't be any worse than hers.

"Pixley's perfectly right," said Ruby. "Daphne will be sitting for Gwendolyn's painting, so Fina can help. And since Flora must take a few hours' break, I'm also available."

Helen's eyes narrowed. "Sir Montague might object ..." Then

her shoulders relaxed. "I'd be most grateful, especially as the pain is worsening. I'll scrounge around upstairs for more aspirin tablets."

We followed Helen downstairs into a narrow corridor, past a larder stuffed with loaves of bread, biscuits, cakes, and scones. Mr Tremore must have brought them over this morning on his boat.

I licked my lips. A little midnight snack wouldn't go amiss.

A vast, modernised kitchen stood at the end of the hallway, complete with hanging copper pans gleaming in the bright overhead lights. The room was partially below ground, so the only ventilation was a small open window. Good thing, too, as the smell of burnt food was strong. Charcoal-covered pies lined the counter.

Helen aimed her ladle at the blackened pies. "Those pies are inedible."

A glance at Ruby confirmed that she also wanted to say, "But they were inedible to begin with."

Instead, we nodded politely.

Pixley unbuttoned and rolled up his sleeves, breaking the awkward silence. "I spotted a cold storage out back. Do we need a key?"

"Fortunately, no. Only John and I have keys this weekend. Even Sir Montague doesn't have his – he sometimes gives his copies to close friends should they want a holiday when he isn't here. But there's not much in the cold storage anyway. I brought all the necessary stores in here since we're due for a storm."

"Perfect. Your kitchen is in good hands, and though we cannot hope to live up to your standards," Pixley said in a clever turn of phrase, "we'll do our best. We'll make a warm and nourishing dish."

Then he made a little shooing motion at Helen.

Helen curved her lips upward, but the pain in her arm made

it a wince rather than a smile. She turned on her heel, marched towards the archway, and halted abruptly. "I appreciate your help. It's been a most trying week."

"Just a moment," said Ruby.

Helen turned around.

"You said 'week'," said Ruby. "What else has happened this week?"

Helen's hair fell over her one eye again. "Oh, did I say week?" She held a hand to her forehead. "This exquisite pain muddles my head."

Without another word, she scurried away.

"Right," said Pixley as soon as her footsteps faded. "I'll see to the larder. You two sit tight."

He padded from the room, humming a little tune.

We were most happy to sit tight, as Pixley was the best cook among us.

Ruby squinted at one of the copper pots hanging on the wall. "Are you thinking what I'm thinking?"

"Perhaps. Perhaps you're thinking Miss Poole is a most careful individual. She wouldn't slip up and say 'week' unless she meant it."

"Mmm..."

"Those marvellous cogs in your brain are spinning furiously," I said. "Is something else bothering you?"

She tapped her teeth. "Well, it's Miss Poole in general. Her lying to us about never having met Dr Rafferty."

"You mean when she brushed her throat?"

She nodded. "Of course, we could be wrong about it, but did you notice what Charles said right before she dropped the glass bowl?"

"I was rather distracted by the room's electric atmosphere," I said.

"Charles said he'd met people pretending to be someone else."

"Well, it could be the obvious interpretation."

"Which is?"

"That she's a nob fallen on hard times."

"Why would that cause her to drop the bowl?"

"Good point. But what difference does it make? We're not on a case—" My heart started to pound. "Are we?"

"Not a murder case, but as far as our other political activities go, I fear the answer is yes."

I stamped my foot. "You promised. You said no more spying until we finish our degrees."

"But I couldn't have guessed they'd follow us. To an island in Cornwall, of all places." She paused. "Not that I know who 'they' is."

"I overheard something in that line." I tapped my foot. "The spying line, I mean."

"In what line?" Pixley's legs buckled under the weight of the largest wheel of cheese I'd ever seen. We rushed forward and helped him heave it onto the worktop.

"Selkies and kelpies! What are you going to do with that?"

Ruby laughed. "Pix did say it would be a nourishing meal."

He caressed the cheese. "Remember when my editor sent me to Switzerland last year?"

"I recall the chocolate you brought for me," I said.

"Yes, well, I'm sorry it was half-melted. But when I spotted this cheese, that's what popped into my mind – melting food. Whilst I was in Bern, the local cheese union served up this divine dish made almost entirely of cheese. They hope it will become popular all over the world."

He scanned the shelves and grabbed a bottle of white wine. "This will do." He handed it to Ruby. "Open it, will you?"

"Gladly. I could use a glass of wine after today." She

squeezed her eyes shut and pulled the cork. The resulting popping sound was most satisfactory.

I handed her three glasses, and she poured generous measures into each.

Pixley rubbed his forehead. "Steady on, Ruby. Save some for the pot!"

Unperturbed, Ruby sipped her wine. "Keep your trousers on. Plenty for all, including your precious pot. Now, tell us the name of this cheese and wine concoction."

"What was it called ..." Pixley peered into his wine glass as if it held the answer. "Ah yes! It's called fondue. We'll have a glorious time eating it."

I ignored the odd ambiguity in his words and lifted my glass in a toast. "To Cutmere Perch, and a better day tomorrow."

"I'll say." Ruby surveyed me with an unnerving stare. "Now, you were going to tell us what you overheard, Feens."

I told them about Charles and Sir Montague's conversation, leaving out the bit about Niall finding me behind the hedge.

"I see," said Ruby. "That means Sir Montague had another reason to invite us here this weekend."

"To spy on us?" asked Pixley.

"To spy on someone," I said. "Though Charles was the instigator. He must be high up in this sugar company if he has the PM's ear."

"Yes ..." Ruby studied her fingernails. "Did you say Sir Montague seemed reluctant?"

"Well, I couldn't see his face, but yes, he sounded exasperated. He seemed a grudging participant in Charles's scheme. Even though they were on friendly terms, Charles appeared to be forcing him."

"Hmm ..." Pixley looked up from his pot. "So, Sir Montague lied when he said he knew nothing about Charles Vane. He is a mysterious bloke, this Mr Vane. And this doppelgänger business with Ian Clavering is most disturbing."

At the mention of Ian's name, Ruby became fixated on the grooves on the ancient wooden table.

"We forgot to tell you, Fina," said Pixley. "Ruby tried to telephone a friend of that blasted blighter, Ian." He thrust his knife down through a thick piece of cheese.

I swiped a piece and popped it into my mouth. The wine was going to my head, creating a pleasant, muzzy feeling. "Let me guess. The friend knew precisely nothing about Mr Charles Vane."

Ruby sighed. "No, he wasn't aware of Ian's whereabouts, or if he had a cousin with a close resemblance to him. But he did say my friend Perry might have a clue."

I put down my glass. "Perry? Who's Perry?"

"Simply a friend."

Pixley's lips were set in a grim "don't ask" line.

With a slightly tipsy tongue, I said, "What are we waiting for?"

"Serpentine Hall has only one telephone," said Ruby, "and it's in the grand hallway. Anyone could overhear us."

I blinked. "It's just occurred to me: why does this island have a telephone at all? How did they manage it?"

Pixley adjusted his spectacles and cleared his throat. "In 1878, Queen Victoria witnessed telephone calls placed by Alexander Graham Bell on the Isle of Wight. To London, that is."

"Aren't you a positive fount of information," I said sourly. History was supposed to be my forte. "Though I still don't understand how."

He waved his hand. "Haven't a clue about the how, dear girl, but as to this island—"

"It must have been a pet project of the previous owner,"

Ruby put in. "He must have had shedloads of cash for the project, and then persuaded the government to allow him to do it."

"But the Isle of Wight is near the mainland. Surely it would be easier there."

"I studied Cutmere Perch on a map." Pixley rubbed one eye. "There wasn't much to do on the train down to Penzance. But I learned the island isn't as far out to sea as it appears."

"That's settled then," said Ruby. "We'll telephone at midnight when no one will be about."

Visions of biscuits and scones from the larder danced in my head. Maybe I'd toddle downstairs for my midnight snack. Right before midnight, of course.

14

"Curse you, Flora! That's my bread!" Daphne leaned over the table, peering into the pot of bubbling cheese, kept on a low flame. Pixley had found a Primus stove in the kitchen and had moved it to the dining table to hold the fondue pot.

"Finder's keepers." Flora piloted the metal skewer with the cheesy bread cube into her mouth. "Delicious!"

I beamed at the gathering – Pixley's fondue idea was a decided triumph. Even Niall and Luca were relaxed.

"Watch your hand, Niall!" called Luca. "You nearly stabbed it."

"Watch your own hand," Niall said sarcastically, before plunging his skewer into the pot again.

I shut my eyes, hoping we wouldn't have yet another accident involving blood and limbs.

"Let's have a round of applause for our most gracious cooks, Miss Dove and Miss Aubrey-Havelock," said Sir Montague. "And an additional serving of gratitude for Mr Hayford, our scurrilous young journalist and chef extraordinaire."

After a few half-hearted tries at our makeshift fondue pot, Sir Montague had retired to the chair at the end of the long table. He was haggard and exhausted but was enjoying himself nonetheless.

The applause died and we all collapsed into the chairs, our stomachs bursting from cheese and bread. At least, mine was.

Instinctively, I accounted for the missing members of our party. Gwendolyn was absent because she was working on her sketch after Daphne had finished her nude posing. Helen was recuperating in her room.

But John. Where was John Benbow?

I held up a finger. "Has anyone seen Mr Benbow? He's missing all the fun, and there's still cheese left."

Charles cocked his head like the mechanical men I'd seen in films. "I saw him after lunch. He was leaving through the front door. I don't know where he was going."

"When I was applying Miss Poole's bandage," said Niall, "he mentioned taking the small boat to St Mary's for more medical supplies. Miss Poole needed more aspirin tablets and a proper dressing." He scratched his head. "It made perfect sense, but now I'm puzzled."

"Why are you puzzled?" asked Flora. "Helen also asked me for aspirin tablets."

"I see what Niall's after," said Luca. "The shops would be closed on St Mary's when he arrived, so where would he buy these supplies?"

"I can answer that," said Sir Montague. "The locals have a barter system after hours. Besides, Dr Samuels, the local GP, is always available for such needs."

"It's curious," said Charles. "After all, I have tablets, and Miss Poole never asked me for any."

"Well, we must not disturb the dear lady," said Sir Montague. "I expect she's already asleep."

"What about Mr Benbow?" asked Pixley.

Sir Montague waved a hand. "John served with me in the Great War and is a most resourceful soldier. I'm certain he's bedding down in St Mary's with a friend tonight and will return in the morning."

∽

FOLLOWING A PLEASANT DINNER, it was time to plunge into a detective story from Serpentine Hall's ample library. I cracked it open and pulled the warm quilt around my chest in my large four-poster bed.

Just as Miss Celestine Rambler's night-time adventures had drawn me into another world, a noise drew my eyes from the page.

A rattling noise.

I held the book in mid-air, straining to listen above the thumping of my heart.

A rush of air from the chimney reinvigorated the dying embers in the fireplace. That peculiar whistling noise from the chimney arose, signalling a gathering storm outside. I shivered and pulled the bedclothes up to my chin. I set down *The Ghost at Minx Hill* on my lap, trying to familiarise myself with the sounds of the oncoming storm. It was foolish to have selected a book about the supernatural from the library. The house must be bursting with ghosties. I much preferred my ghosts to be the friendly kind – the ones who tap you on the shoulder and tell you where to search for the buried treasure.

Bump.

There it was again. No mistaking it this time. And it didn't match the whooshing of the fireplace; more like an open shutter banging outside.

The moon shone briefly, illuminating the clock on my bedside table. Half eleven. Everyone was tired from a day of travel and mishaps. Our overindulgence in cheese and wine might have helped too.

Ruby and Pixley agreed we'd meet downstairs by the telephone at midnight. We planned to ring Ruby's friend Perry to learn more about the mysterious Charles Vane.

My stomach rumbled, answering the first low booming of thunder outside. Perhaps I'd nip down to the larder and have an almost-midnight snack before we made the telephone call. And perhaps that disconcerting noise would have disappeared by the time I returned.

I threw back the bedcovers and drew on my dressing gown.

Opting for socks rather than slippers, I glided across the smooth wooden floor, through the well-oiled door, and down the stairs. I averted my gaze from the ancestral portraits staring at me in the moonlight.

I tiptoed into the empty, dark corridor, where branches waved their shadows on the walls, sending the occasional scratching noise against the windowpane of the conservatory in front of me. The wind died down, bringing a welcome moment of silence.

The noise came from my right, down the hallway. I soon dismissed it as a tree branch and turned to go downstairs.

The creaking, scraping noise returned. I froze, not from fear but indecision. Should I take a peek?

My curiosity won out over the midnight snack. After all, I'd have a nibble after we telephoned Ruby's friend.

A shaft of light from Sir Montague's studio lit up a sliver of the hallway, so I padded towards it. Then I heard more than a creak.

I heard voices.

Squinting through the crack from the open door, I spotted Sir Montague at his desk, holding a painting of a coal miner. The miner's smudged face held a singular, watchful expression.

Even from this vantage point, it was a striking portrait – one resembling a photograph rather than a painting.

A white, translucent hand motioned across the canvas. Luca.

"It's marvellous," he said. "The best yet. We'll sell it in a flash."

Flora's head appeared, bending over the painting. "Luca's right. And no one will ever know."

"They'd better not," said Luca. "Do we have the same bargain as ever?"

"We do," sighed Sir Montague. His hand dropped to his side, signalling exhaustion. Or resignation.

"Right," said Luca. "You two can go. I'll stay – I must check a few things with the painting."

Something tickled my neck. I brushed my fingers against it, realising the hairs did stick up on one's neck, exactly like Lady Wingfield's encounter with the spirit world in *The Ghost at Minx Hill*.

Like Lady Wingfield, I had the distinct impression someone was behind me.

Be brave, Fina, be brave.

And so, with one eye open and one closed, I craned my neck behind me.

15

Thank goodness. It was Ruby crouching down and edging along the wall, so I tiptoed after her into the dark.

Behind me, the main staircase creaked and groaned under hurried footsteps making their way down.

We weren't the only ones itching for a midnight roam around Serpentine Hall.

I turned my head towards the stairs as we flattened against the wall.

Charles Vane emerged from the gloom, cinching his white dressing gown with grim determination. He turned into the library. It was doubtful he was seeking a bedtime reading companion – everyone knew going to the library was a clever ruse, though for what purpose was unclear.

I waved Ruby into the study on our left. Once inside, she shut the door and pressed against it. "It's quite the party out there, with everyone rattling about the house. Perhaps the storm has set everyone on edge. I'm rather restless myself."

"Who else did you spot – other than Charles?"

"I didn't see Daphne, but the light was on underneath her door. Niall's light was also on, next to her bedroom."

"He's in the Burgundy room?"

"Yes. Another excellent colour choice by Miss Poole."

"But you didn't see them?"

"No, but I heard soft laughter coming from Daphne's room."

"So she was snickering to herself? If I were her, I suppose I'd find myself amusing."

"I heard a man chuckling."

My stomach churned. Other than Pixley, Sir Montague was in the studio, and John Benbow was presumably snoozing in St Mary's. Charles did go to the library, but maybe he'd left Daphne's room as Ruby came downstairs. No, I had to face it: the most likely candidate was Niall.

"Feens? Are you there, Feens?"

"Ah, sorry. I was thinking."

"You do that a lot."

"There's so much to consider."

"It's true. I often feel my head walks around by itself, just thinking."

"At least your grey cells produce results!"

The doorknob turned, and Pixley's well-shod shoe slipped in through the crack.

"I can hear you two from the hallway," he scolded, though in an indulgent tone.

"How did you plan to ring up this Perry character?" I asked, pointing towards the hallway. "That telephone lacks any privacy."

"It's almost as if it's on purpose," said Pixley.

"Precisely." Ruby tapped her teeth. "So there must be another telephone somewhere."

"Ah, I see your point," I said. "A house this size must have two telephones, and it's logical that the second one is in the study."

We searched the room, moving aside the heavy oak furniture and opening drawers.

Pixley pressed his body against a bookcase.

"What are you doing?" I asked. "Taking a rest?"

"Searching for a secret passage, of course."

I smiled. Pixley's imagination was nearly as fertile as my own.

"Hey presto!" Ruby hissed, pointing to a tiny cupboard door built into the bookcase. A shiny black telephone sat inside.

"Well, go on," said Pixley. "With everyone wandering around like restless cats, someone's certain to pop in here sooner rather than later."

Ruby held up a finger. "Hello, I'd like to make a trunk call, please. Limehouse 6469. Yes, I'll wait."

I hoisted myself onto the gargantuan oak desk as it was the only free seat in the room. As I leaned back, propping myself up with my arms, my hand slipped on a piece of paper.

Must be yet another bill. Sir Montague had a lot of those.

It was an invoice, but not one for the greengrocers or another mundane necessity. The return address was Niall Rafferty's clinic in Harley Street. The fact that Niall catered to such wealthy clients surprised me. He was such a contrarian and Harley Street was a conventional – though certainly lucrative – choice.

The typed invoice was for a one-hour session without a client's name or date. Perhaps that was to protect Sir Montague's anonymity. After all, no one wanted their name associated with a psychotherapist.

"Hello, Perry? It's Ruby," she whispered. "I'm terribly sorry to ring so late." She held the receiver at an angle so we could listen in.

Perry croaked, "Anything for you, Ruby."

I'd never heard of this Perry chap, even though Ruby and I

practically lived in each other's pockets. Though she had kept her new cottage in Oxford a secret for a few weeks.

"Perry, you remember Ian, don't you? Ian Clavering?"

"A scurrilous cad who left you in the lurch. Ruby, I cannot understand what you see in him. Why, I'm twice the—"

"Of course, but this is urgent. It's business. Where is Ian? How can we contact him?"

A pause followed. "I haven't seen him for at least six months. You know how it is. Once the blighter disappears, that's it. There's no tracing him."

Ruby groaned.

Pixley gently wrestled the receiver from her and held it to his ear. He adjusted his spectacles, as if he were about to meet Perry in person. "Perry. It's Pixley Hayford here. Yes, yes. From the *Daily Rumble*. We met at Marco's, remember?"

Pause. "Quite a bash, wasn't it? Look here, you might help us given your varied connections. Have you ever heard of a bloke named Charles Vane?"

Pause. "From Barbados. Supposedly works for a sugar company."

Pixley put his hand over the receiver. "What's his company called?"

"Ledburn and Lamport," I said.

"Yes, Perry. It's Ledburn and Lamport. Listen, this Vane cove bears a striking resemblance to that perennial absentee, Ian. Actually, he told me he's Ian's half-brother."

Ruby gasped, and for the second time that day, she dug her nails into my arm. Charles was Ian's half-brother? It was possible, though I didn't recall Ian ever mentioning a half-brother.

"I see, I see," said Pixley. "Yes. Well, thanks for your help."

He put down the receiver and blew out his cheeks. "Sorry. I forgot to tell you I grilled young Vane, and he said he was Ian's half-brother. And before you say anything, it isn't true. Perry said it was a bald-faced lie. To put it politely."

I snorted, disgusted on Ruby's behalf. "The nerve."

But Ruby's face had taken on a wistful, dreamlike look. "Perhaps Perry simply wasn't aware of this half-brother. Ian might be embarrassed by having a brother who works for sugar barons,"

Ruby hummed under her breath, "Brother, brother, brother."

Pixley frowned at me. I'd only seen Ruby like this when she had received a postcard from Ian. Surely she hadn't fallen for this imitation Ian? Was she imagining herself as Mrs Charles Vane? Impossible.

"What else did Perry say?" I asked.

Pixley rubbed his handkerchief over his bald head. "He'd never heard of Charles Vane, and Perry knows everyone. He keeps a watch on large companies in the Caribbean since it's a tense situation at the moment."

"Well?" asked Ruby dreamily. "Is there anything else?"

"I'm afraid so," he said. "I caught a distinct 'click' right before ringing off. One of our friends in Serpentine Hall has been listening in."

16

The storm had whipped itself into a positive fury, battering the windows and doors of Serpentine Hall. Despite the terrific noise, the building's low height and sprawling wings could withstand a hurricane. This meant it also had long corridors, which were less than ideal for snooping. Not that we were snooping, of course.

After we'd completed our telephone task, Ruby pressed open the study door with one finger and peered out. Just as she slipped through, a gust of wind buffeted the windows and sent a cold stream of air around my head.

I flipped up the collar of my dressing gown, wishing it had a hood attached. It was all distinctly unnerving.

When we reached the staircase, Pixley motioned us downstairs. Without stopping to ask why, Ruby and I slid our hands down the marble bannisters, following him into the gloom. He switched on the corridor light and moved towards the kitchen.

I hurried along, grateful that there might be a midnight snack after all. Perhaps I'd nip into the larder first, gather my sandwich supplies, and prepare it in the kitchen. My tongue tingled in anticipation.

Ruby and Pixley disappeared behind the green baise kitchen door whilst I turned left, into the larder. I fumbled for the light switch, finally finding it near the door.

I flicked it once, twice, and then once more. Nothing happened.

Crumbs. The light from the corridor wasn't strong enough.

Vowing I'd rectify this problem, I retreated to the kitchen. Ruby was stirring a pot on the stove, humming as she did so.

"Cocoa," she said simply.

"Good for the nerves," said Pixley.

"My stomach is demanding more than cocoa. Have either of you a torch?"

"No, but I received this spiffing lighter last week." Pixley withdrew a silver cigarette lighter from his pocket, caressing it with his thumb.

"Which lover gave it to you?" asked Ruby.

"Most amusing, Miss Dove. If you must know, Pipsqueak Purloin gave it to me since he has oodles of cash and was coveting a new one encrusted with diamonds."

"Well, thanks to Pipsqueak, I can have a snack," I said.

Pixley tossed me the lighter.

Back in the larder, I waved the steady flame into one corner, illuminating a heap of round bread loaves and a few lonely scones under glass. Scones. It would be much simpler than making a sandwich.

Moving towards the scones, my leg bumped into a sack of flour. I nudged it out of the way, determined to capture my quarry.

I held the lighter in one hand as I nibbled the chewy scone.

In the middle of the room, I hit another sack.

How could efficient Helen Poole allow bags of flour to lounge all over the floor? John, too, was a military man. Wouldn't he keep things in apple-pie order?

I decided to help them since John had disappeared and Helen had a bad arm. So I set down my scone and balanced the lighter on a low stool.

The flame cast shadows over the stool and the floor. I bent over, my fingers grasping for prickly sacking material.

Instead, they brushed something soft and silken. Even squishy.

I moved the lighter closer to the floor and stifled a scream in my throat.

Those weren't sacks of flour.

∼

ALL I REMEMBER IS STARING into those fishlike blue eyes.

Ruby and Pixley burst into the larder, yanking me up from the floor.

"I'll be a—" Pixley clamped his mouth shut. Ruby's hands flew to her face.

"I-I-I just found him like this, sprawled out."

"Here, Feens." Ruby held out a hand. "Come over here."

I took her hand and let her guide me to the doorway. My legs tingled and my hands quivered. Ruby put her shawl around me as she had when I'd tumbled into the sea.

"She's in shock," said Ruby.

"We're all in shock," breathed Pixley.

Whilst Ruby and I had seen our fair share of bodies, Pixley had seen even more as a newspaperman. He rubbed his forefinger over pursed lips and stared at the body. "Sir Montague must have had a bad turn."

"A bad turn?" I hissed. "This isn't a Victorian melodrama. It's real life. He's dead."

Ruby squeezed my shoulder. "Look here, none of us are

thinking clearly. Maybe his heart did stop – after all, he was the right age for it."

"Perhaps he was so overwhelmed by his pastry choices that he died from pure delight!" I whinnied uncontrollably, shaking all over. My mind told me to stop, but my body had other plans.

Pixley cradled my face in his hands. "Red. Snap out of it!"

His loud, barking command worked, though it also roused the household. Scurrying footsteps and shuffling soon came from above.

We looked at each other. With my newfound sobriety, I said, "We've done nothing wrong. We simply came down for cocoa and a snack, a perfectly normal occupation during a weekend house party. I found Sir Montague as I was foraging for a bite to eat."

During my lecture, Ruby had been inspecting the body, an irrepressible habit of hers. She guided the flame up and down his body and then scooped up something from the floor, flinging it into her pocket.

"What did you—?" I asked.

But it was too late. The others had arrived.

17

Our trio huddled in the drawing room, sipping cold cups of cocoa in front of a wheezing fire. The storm still raged outside with a rare ferocity, but I was impervious to the bumps, thumps, and screeching. My mind was a blank canvas, and I'd soon finished my cocoa, tasting nothing at all.

"Dear Red, don't be morbid." Pixley patted my hand. "We've seen death before, and at least it was from natural causes."

Ruby's eyes narrowed as she stared into the flames.

"Penny for your thoughts?" I asked Ruby.

She propped up her head with one hand on the settee. "I'm not as sanguine as Pix about natural causes."

"I'd scarcely call myself sanguine," said Pixley.

She flipped a pencil through her fingers, one by one. "Sorry, my brain is a bit scrambled. There was something peculiar about Sir Montague's face. Or was it his body?" She closed her eyes.

I closed mine, too, conjuring the ghastly image of Sir Montague sprawled on the floor. But nothing struck me as significant.

"Talking of peculiar," said Pixley, "what did you find in the larder?"

"Ah! Thank you for reminding me." Ruby reached into her pocket and held out a rectangular scrap of paper, torn on three sides.

"It's a telephone number," she said. "Southampton 7415."

"Do you think the number is significant?" I asked.

"Probably not," said Ruby.

"You'll try the telephone number anyway, won't you?" Pixley chuckled. "Always after a mystery."

"It has been a mysterious weekend," I countered. "My fall – or push – into the sea? This dubious Vane character? That conversation in the conservatory between Charles and Sir Montague? And the scene in his studio with Flora and Luca?"

"The painting contest itself is a rum idea," Pixley murmured, adding to my catalogue of oddities.

Ruby leaned forward. "What scene between Flora and Luca, Feens?"

Just as I'd finished my story about the studio, Gwendolyn burst into the room.

"Well, that's torn it," she said in a rare lapse into a colloquialism. With her hands behind her back, she hunched over and trotted to the fire, resembling a mischievous brownie or other tiny house spirit. She stood with her back to us, warming her hands. Then she spun round. "The sabotage is complete. Utterly complete."

Flora stumbled into the drawing room, one hand rubbing her eye. Daphne trailed behind her. In their gossamer blue and scarlet peignoirs, they floated about the room like gently waving jellyfish. Daphne, however, soon crumpled herself up in a chair and closed her eyes.

Flora blinked, still processing Gwendolyn's words. "I must have misheard you, Gwendolyn. What did you say?"

"Sabotage, I said. The plot against me is complete. Sir Montague is dead, the contest is over, and I shall never recapture my rights to that painting, nor restore my reputation."

"Our mentor died, and all you can think of is yourself?"

Gwendolyn cocked her head. "He was a great man, but everyone's time comes. It might be an hour, a day, or sixty years."

With her tiny hand balling into a fist, Flora jerked forward, flinging herself at Gwendolyn. Ruby jumped up and blocked the furious figure just inches away from Gwendolyn.

Flora reeled back a step, smashing her fist into her own hand. But her eyes blazed.

Given my short stature, I found the stand-off between these two tiny women rather amusing.

"Gwendolyn Brice." Flora lowered her voice. "You're the most sanctimonious, self-centred, astorperious, dried-up, useless little has-been, or better yet, never-was, I've ever met."

"Pah!" spat out Gwendolyn in her usual outdated language. "At least I'm not a toadying sycophantic lickspittle who would paint their own mother as a devil if a buyer waved a pound note in front of their nose."

Flora took one step forward. "Ha! That's what a loser always says." She held her fists to her eyes in a mock crying motion. "'Look at sad little me. My titled rich parents rejected me, leaving me to be raised by dirt-poor Welsh bumpkins.'"

Gwendolyn launched forward and slapped Flora across the face.

"Ladies!" Pixley rose.

Luca padded in, scratching his spiky blond hair. "Charles and Niall are still downstairs. Niall's the closest we have to a doctor, so he's inspecting the body. The only person unaccounted for is Helen." As he counted on his fingers, I noticed the tip of one had a sticking plaster.

"You're right," said Pixley. "Shouldn't Helen have risen by now? The noise we've been making would raise the dead."

"Really, Mr Hayford," said Gwendolyn. Was her scolding prompted by her own feelings of embarrassment? Her earlier outburst was rather selfish.

Pixley covered his mouth. "Sorry. Sometimes my mouth can run faster than my brain."

"Pixley's right," said Ruby. "Miss Poole ought to have joined us by now."

"Maybe she took a bit too much sleeping draught." Flora shuddered. "If I had a gash in my arm, I might do just that."

"All the same," said Ruby, "I'll look in on her. Just to be sure she's not ill."

18

Relieved to leave behind the tension in the drawing room, our trio made a beeline for Helen's Viridian bedroom upstairs.

"I say, Miss Brice's mind is almost as conspiratorial as my own," said Pixley. "Is it simply her personality?"

I recalled our painting session together. "It's difficult to say. She certainly has a sharp mind and notices things – as she said herself, she's a keen observer."

"So she wouldn't let anyone pull Welsh wool over her eyes," said Pixley.

"But she has a vivid imagination, so she could easily become detached from reality," I said.

"What say you, Ruby?" asked Pixley. "Do you fancy that Flora's insults about Gwendolyn's upbringing are true?"

Ruby stopped and lifted her head. "Flora did tell me that Gwendolyn and her brother were abandoned."

"A sad but not uncommon phenomenon," said Pixley.

"Quite so, but they didn't discover they were orphans until they were adults."

I snapped my fingers. "There's only one photograph in

Gwendolyn's room, and I'm certain it's of her and her brother as children."

Pixley rubbed his chin. "Discovering you were actually an orphan would be a surprise. But would you then suspect every person you met of trying to sabotage you?"

"Don't exaggerate, dear Pix," said Ruby. "It's not as bad as all that."

"Pix is right about one thing. You'd start to question people's motives," I said. "Besides, if she believed her real parents were rich, her childhood poverty might make her bitter."

Ruby knocked on Helen's door, but the storm's terrific eldritch scream drowned out her soft tapping. Then she smoothed her hair and skirt and banged her fist against the door. So hard that the Viridian canvas tumbled to the floor.

Despite the grim situation, I stifled a chuckle at Ruby's sudden assault on the door.

"It's no good," said Pixley. "We must break down the door."

"But if she took a sleeping draught, she probably cannot hear us knocking." I waved at the windows. "Who could sleep through this gale? Maybe we ought to leave her alone since there's only dreadful news awaiting her when she awakes."

We turned to Ruby.

"I have a third solution," she said. "John has the other set of keys. Let's see if he left them in his bedroom."

"Surely he would have taken them with him," I said.

"Perhaps he left them so Helen had a spare set," said Pixley.

Ruby shrugged. "Let's have a gander. Now, what colour was John's room?"

"Cobalt," said Pixley. "Spot on for his personality, I'd say. Steady, calm, and loyal. I've seen enough of Mr Benbow to make that assessment."

I had to agree. Mr Benbow was the most even-keeled person at Serpentine Hall.

"Here we are." Pixley turned the knob. "Voilà!"

John Benbow's room was a perfect square, and everything inside reflected this sensibility. Chairs were pushed into their proper place, and several pairs of expensive but worn shoes were lined carefully along the wall. The counterpane had been tightened on the bed with military precision, and even the pens on the desk were lined up to attention.

Through the window above his desk, a lighthouse from another island pulsed in the darkness, bringing a sense of calm.

Pixley rummaged in the desk drawers, and I studied the stack of papers on the blotting pad. On the first sheet, a pound sign caught my eye. This house was positively awash in receipts.

This receipt was for a Finch Gallery painting purchased by John Benbow. And not just for any painting.

I held up the receipt. "Listen to this. John Benbow purchased a painting for three hundred pounds from the Finch Gallery a week ago."

Pixley whistled. "I could use three hundred pounds, but how does it help us find the keys?"

"Wait." I ignored Pixley. "It was for the portrait of the coal miner I saw in Sir Montague's studio."

Ruby looked up. "I'm with Pix. What gives, Feens?"

"Don't you see?" I was frustrated until I spotted the clock on the wall. It was four o'clock in the morning, so no wonder I was tongue-tied.

With a deep breath, I tried again. "Flora, Luca, and Sir Montague were discussing this very painting of a coal miner."

"Quite a coincidence," said Ruby, "given the coal loader strike in St Lucia."

"Sir Montague had painted it, though, so why would John Benbow have a receipt purchasing it from Luca a week ago?"

Pixley scratched his head. "That is a puzzle."

"Found it!" Ruby held up a tangle of keys.

In our excitement, we left aside the receipt puzzle and returned to Helen's door. After a few false starts, one key produced a satisfying clunk.

Pixley opened the door and tiptoed in.

"Miss Poole?" he called softly.

Ruby switched on the light. Helen was turned on her side in bed, facing the wall.

Gripped by a sudden sense of propriety, Pixley moved backwards and waved us towards the bed.

"Does she have a fever?" I pointed to the red flush across her cheeks.

Ruby's brows furrowed. "Miss Poole? Helen? Time to wake up."

I tugged on Helen's emerald silk sleeve with little result. So I pulled a bit harder.

Miss Poole suddenly flopped over on her back. Her lips were parted, but her eyes remained shut.

Ruby flung back the bedclothes and grasped Helen's thin arm.

"Quickly! Find her pulse!"

I put two fingers on Helen's wrist and closed my eyes. "Yes," I breathed. "It's faint, but she has a pulse."

"Thank goodness." Ruby lifted one of Helen's eyelids. "She's been drugged, by herself..."

"Or by someone else," said Pixley.

"Now who's being morbid?" I asked.

"Perhaps you're right," said Pixley. "Perhaps it's yet another coincidence. Helen was under a great strain and maybe she was distracted. Hence the overdose."

Ruby stared at her hands and then rubbed her nose. "Pix is right. It's probably a coincidence."

"There!" I said. "You just rubbed your nose."

Ruby arched an eyebrow. "And?"

"Jupiter's teeth!" exclaimed Pixley. "Don't you remember, Ruby? You only rub your nose when you're lying. Since it's a subconscious gesture, you must not believe your own words."

"But I do believe what I said. At least ... Maybe it's a case for Dr Rafferty. Shall I ask him to examine my head? Or my subconscious, rather?"

A soft tap came from the door.

"Be with you in a minute," I called, running and pulling it open.

Niall stood in a black dressing gown with his hands deep in his pockets. Upon seeing me, his thick eyebrows lifted.

"Miss Aubrey-Havelock?" He gazed past me into the room. "And Mr Hayford and Miss Dove. Well, I'm glad I found you here as well."

Ruby peeked over my shoulder. "Why 'as well'?"

His eyes softened. "Is Helen ill?"

"She's been drugged," said Ruby. "She must have had too much of a sleeping draught, but I expect she'll recover."

His accent sharpened. "Well, at least there's that, then."

"Look here," said Pixley. "What's the matter?"

Niall squared his jaw and surveyed each of us. "I had a closer look at Sir Montague. His body, I mean."

"Was it a heart attack, as we suspected?" I asked.

"He didn't die of natural causes."

"Was he poisoned?" asked Pixley.

Ruby gasped, holding a hand to her forehead. "I've remembered what was bothering me. One of the flour sacks was stained, but I couldn't see the colour of it in the dark. Was it blood?"

"It was definitely blood." Niall ran his hand through his tangled hair. "I'm not one for pretty speeches, so I'll simply say it. Someone stuck a metal skewer through the back of Sir Montague's neck."

19

The next few hours were a blur. The storm had weakened to a whistling moan but had been strong enough to cut the telephone line. Gwendolyn had discovered this when she tried to phone the police. She'd planned to tell them that Sir Montague's murder was part of a plot to discredit her.

Ruby and I stood in the portrait gallery overlooking a rose-coloured sunrise with luminescent clouds and single shafts of light onto the sea. A jackdaw flew past, twisting and turning in the wind, finally surrendering and letting the wind carry him out to sea.

Though the dawn was serene, my nerves were not. So I reached for the familiar. "Fancy a cup of tea?"

Ruby's face drooped, but her eyes sparkled. A sure sign the gears were turning in that extraordinary brain of hers.

"Tea! What a smashing plan, Feens. Where do you find such ideas?"

"Well, I-I-I ..." I was taken aback by her enthusiasm. Especially since it required passing the larder.

She shot through the door. "Pixley's asleep upstairs, so let's let him rest."

My legs flew after her, struggling to keep up.

Charles Vane came into view on the stairs above. "I say, are you two making tea? I'm craving a cuppa." Unlike my dishevelled state, Charles Vane was in perfect working order. True, his hair was so short that he couldn't look dishevelled if he tried, and his skin was an even light-brown tone, without a speck of imperfection. But the real miracle was the spotless condition of his white dressing gown. I could never achieve such a feat.

"Make your own tea!" Ruby called back to him.

"Why is Ruby in such a rush?" he asked me.

"Ah, women's issues, you know." It was the best I could do.

Charles grimaced and nodded like a man of the world. "Right. Erm, right." He cinched his belt and disappeared.

With that obstacle cleared from my path, I descended the stairs slowly. Taking one measured step at a time, I approached the larder, knowing that's where Ruby would be.

She crouched on the floor. "Don't worry, we'll make tea soon."

I stared at the empty space now lit by a lamp someone had moved into the larder. "Where's Sir Montague?"

"Before you came downstairs, I had a nip around. I spotted him in the billiard room down the hall."

"Billiard room?" I asked.

"I expect Niall and the others moved the body there because it's cool. To keep the body—"

"Ah yes, I see." I clapped my hands together, too nauseated to hear any more. "Well, that's that. What did you wish to see?"

"Will you help me with something?"

"If you tell me what it is."

"Trust me."

Groaning, I moved into the doorway, averting my eyes from the floor and concentrating on the now less-than-appetising food on the counter.

"You agree we found the body face-up?"

I nodded.

"And his feet were facing the door?"

"Yes."

She stepped gingerly around the larder, murmuring, "The police will have a fit over the body being moved."

"Thank goodness they're not here to complain."

She pointed at the walls. "The room can only hold one person in it. Or two, if they're embracing."

"Is that important?"

"It means the murderer had to be facing Sir Montague, or standing directly behind him."

I examined the U-shaped counters lining the larder. Once inside, it was easier to move backwards rather than to turn around.

"You're right," I said. "But he couldn't have been facing the murderer since they struck the back of his neck."

"Correct. Suppose the murderer didn't move the body after committing the murder. In that case, the culprit was standing directly behind Sir Montague when she or he attacked him." Ruby lifted her arm and brought it down in a hammering motion.

"The murderer would be squeezed like a sardine. Behind Sir Montague, that is," I said. "Both would face forward."

"As if one was a driver and the other was a back-seat passenger." Ruby tapped her teeth. "Why would they be in such an awkward position?"

She pointed at a bloodstain snaking along the tiled floor. "And another thing. The floor should have more blood on it."

The horror of the crime still lingered, but my brain was slowly switching itself on. "The murder was rather surgical. Maybe the skewer stopped the blood flow."

Ruby wrinkled her brow. "Very good, Feens. You might have something there."

Encouraged, I rattled on. "Or was Sir Montague moved here after the murder? That would explain the lack of blood and the odd positioning of the body."

Flora's head popped in the doorway, but she studiously avoided looking inside. "Am I interrupting? I came down to make tea. Would you like a cup?"

"Ra-ther," said Ruby. "We were simply testing out a little theory."

"Oh?" Flora shivered. "Do you mind talking in the kitchen? This room gives me the horrors."

We followed her into the kitchen. Flora's usually lively step had vanished, replaced by a sad little shuffle, interrupted by an occasional hop on the ball of her foot.

I lit a match and put on the large, ancient kettle, busying myself with the normality that comes with tea. I placed cheerful flowered crockery on a tray and hunted for a packet of biscuits.

"It's so horrible." Flora sat and jiggled her leg. It could have been nervous energy. Or it could have been nervousness.

"Indeed." Ruby bowed her head in a sympathetic gesture. "On a brighter note, Helen Poole is fine, and we must hope John Benbow will return soon."

"When does Mr Tremore ferry supplies to us?" I asked.

"Last time I was here, he only came on the Monday," said Flora. "Helen might know more about it. When she wakes up."

Ruby sat across from Flora, her hand propping up her chin. "Whilst we're waiting for tea, would you share your theories about Sir Montague?"

"I just can't think." As if waking from a nightmare, she ran her hands over her eyes. "Who would kill him? Why? And like that? It's so gruesome."

I dropped a few heaped spoons of tea into the pot, inhaling

the calming, earthy smell. "It's such a bizarre way to kill someone."

"They must have been desperate," said Flora.

"Or in a rage," said Ruby.

The tea kettle whistled.

Ruby hitched her chair closer to Flora. "Tell us what you really think. Maybe closing your eyes will help."

Flora did, but her eyelids flickered. The woman had so much electricity running through her veins that she simply couldn't keep her eyes shut.

"Good," said Ruby, her voice taking on a soothing tone. "When you heard the news, what was your first thought?"

Flora's eyelids stopped pulsing. "Charles Vane."

"Why?" I asked.

"Because he's the only person I hadn't met before."

"You sounded like you had other people in your head," said Ruby.

Flora coughed. "Gwendolyn and Luca. Gwendolyn, because it means the contest is over and I clearly would have won. As for Luca, I'm not confident he's playing above board. It's perfectly normal for art dealers to engage in a few questionable activities, but Luca sails too close to the wind."

I placed two cups of tea on the table, wondering how Flora would explain her secretive conversation with Sir Montague and Luca in the studio.

Pixley walked in, rubbing his hands. "I say, I'm ready for tea."

I waved him to the tea kettle, trying to divert him so Flora wouldn't stop talking.

Her words had halted, though she did mouth "forgery" in Ruby's direction.

Good Lord. Forgery? I wasn't shocked by this given Luca's already questionable behaviour, but how did it relate to murder?

I handed Pixley a cup of tea. "We were discussing the tragedy with Flora."

But Flora had sped out of the room, carrying her rattling teacup as she fled.

"You do have a way of interrupting, Pix," said Ruby.

"Sorry, but I was gasping for a cup. Besides, Flora is your friend and partner in crime, isn't she? Surely she'll spill the beans for you."

"I'm not confident of that, though she hinted that Luca was involved in some rather dodgy practices."

"Such as forgery?" asked Pixley airily.

My mouth dropped open. "How did you know?"

Pixley emptied the cow creamer into his teacup. "Had a chat with Gwendolyn and she said Luca specialised in forgery."

Ruby chuckled. "Any other headlines from our morning reporter?"

"Niall's tighter-lipped than a clam at low tide. Though I expect he's bound by a professional code."

Pixley set down his teacup. "I also spoke to Daphne, who was the opposite of Niall. She was a positive fount of words, though I found few of them useful."

"Go on," I said. "She must believe it's a conspiracy, like Gwendolyn."

Pixley lowered his voice. "Not really. No, she believes—"

"Hello, darlings." Daphne's voice echoed down the hallway.

Daphne whirled into the kitchen. She'd added a scarlet kimono on top of her floaty bit of nonsense, creating an effect unique to Daphne Wandesford. "I'm dreadfully thirsty. For tea, that is. And perhaps a biscuit?"

I pressed a teacup into her hand and refilled the cow creamer. "I'm afraid all the biscuits are in the larder."

Pixley raised his cup in Daphne's direction. "The tea's delicious. Add extra milk and it will be exactly like eating a biscuit."

Daphne followed his lead, turning the brown liquid to white. "Mmm ... You're right. Just what I needed after last night."

Daphne sat and patted Ruby with her large, comforting hand. "Dear Ruby, I understand you found the body."

"Actually, I found it," I said defensively.

"But darling Ruby is the sleuth, isn't she?" She gazed into Ruby's eyes whilst her little finger traced a pattern on Ruby's hand.

Pixley raised his eyebrows as far as they would go.

Ruby gently removed Daphne's hand. But she had few qualms about putting Daphne's flirtations to good use. All for a good cause, of course.

Ruby's voice lowered an octave. "Tell us who did it."

Daphne's large, pool-like eyes widened even further. "Well ..." She hesitated only a second before words tumbled forth.

"It was John Benbow. The man is former military. And though he disappeared yesterday, he actually hid on this island, lying in wait. Can't you just see him? I picture him clenching a dagger between his teeth. As he approaches Serpentine Hall, his dagger glints in the moonlight—"

"He was killed with a skewer," I said.

"And he hid on the island during that terrific storm?" asked Pixley.

Daphne waved her hand as if we were irritating gnats. "He was in the military. If needed, he could build a house out of empty tins."

I repressed a laugh.

"Go on." Ruby was now gazing back adoringly at Daphne. My goodness, she was laying it on with a palette knife.

Glowing at her audience of one, Daphne clutched Ruby's hands. "John would lie in wait. He's familiar with all the nooks and crannies, so the job would be simple."

"But why did John kill Sir Montague?" asked Pixley. "I thought he fought alongside Sir Montague in the Great War. He was devoted to the man."

"Ah, that's it!" Daphne slapped the table. "John Benbow has stood in the shadow of Sir Montague ever since he saved John's life during a nasty barrage in 1913. He's felt beholden to him for over twenty years."

"Where did you hear this?" I asked.

"You are direct, aren't you?" Daphne's voice tinkled. "My father was great friends with Sir Montague, so I've known John Benbow for a long time. But not intimately, you understand."

Her eyes flickered in Ruby's direction at the word "intimately".

"So your idea is that John finally chucked it in," said Pixley. "Playing second fiddle, I mean."

"It's a stretch, Daphne," said Ruby. "Even if it were true, why commit murder now? With all these people in the house?"

"And why in such a vicious way?" I put in.

Daphne's bangles clinked against the table. "Fina is spot-on. It being a crime of repressed emotion." Her eyes suddenly lit up. "That's it! Why didn't I think of it before? John Benbow was in love with Sir Montague. He's had a hidden pash for him for years, and finally, unable to endure it any longer, he takes Sir Montague's life and escapes. Or kills himself in a fit of remorse."

"By throwing himself off a cliff high atop Cutmere Perch?" Pixley drummed his fingers on the table.

"Yes, darling!" she gushed, staring into space. "I can see it all now – it would make a fabulous play."

"Except it isn't a play, Daphne," I said. "It's quite real."

20

Pixley blew out his cheeks as Daphne left the kitchen. "One can only take dear Daphne in small doses. I'm glad she gives money to the cause, but blimey, she's a bit much."

"Daphne is rather enthusiastic," said Ruby dryly. "Let's peek in the studio. I expect everyone returned to bed – or at least to their bedrooms."

The house was preternaturally quiet on this calm and foggy morning. Ruby was probably right about everyone being asleep. Except, perhaps, the murderer.

The studio door stood open, but the air in the room was oppressive.

Reading my mind, Pixley unlatched a window, letting in a gush of air.

"Pix!" Ruby pounced on papers fluttering from the desk.

"Sorry." He relatched the window. "The room was stale."

He snatched a curled-up photograph from the floor and smoothed it on the desk. "Hullo, what have we here?"

"That's the coal miner painting I saw last night!"

"All right, all right, Red. What's the fuss about?" asked Pixley.

"It's a photograph of a painting. Even I can see it's an excellent painting, but what's so unusual about it?"

"You're right, Pix. Why should I be excited?" My voice fell.

"On the contrary." Ruby squinted at the photograph. "I can make out the placard hanging next to the painting." She moved to the window, holding it up to the light and then handing it to me. "You have the best eyesight, Feens. What does it say?"

My eyes focused on the typescript. "W-e-n-n-a. Wenna."

"Who is Wenna?" asked Ruby.

"Wenna, Wenna. I've heard that before." I closed my eyes. "Bingo! We were on holiday in Cornwall near Looe on the coast. My brother and I stumbled on a tiny stone church – the church of St Wenna!"

Ruby and Pixley stared at me.

"How the devil did you remember that?" asked Pixley.

"Remember Feens's talent for taking photographs with her memory?"

"Ah yes, the great and wondrous Red." He tapped a pencil on the desk. "I have a theory about the signature. Children have difficulty pronouncing certain letters, like the G in Gwen. Doesn't 'Wenna' sound like 'Gwenna'?"

Ruby slapped her forehead. "Well done, you two! Wenna must derive from Gwendolyn."

"But why doesn't Gwendolyn simply sign with her real name?" I asked.

"Maybe she's trying out a new name for a new type of painting?" asked Ruby.

Pixley slapped his knee. "So Gwendolyn's theory about a plot against her is true – in a sense. Sir Montague steals her paintings, and she flies into a rage and kills him. Bob's your..." He looked at me.

I smiled. "Uncle."

"It's a neat theory," said Ruby.

"But you're not convinced."

"It's not that. I'm thinking of Flora's last word to us in the kitchen."

"Forgery?" I asked.

"We'll ask Flora more about it." She scanned the walls. "Talking of which, where is that coal miner painting in the photograph?"

"Sir Montague was holding it on his desk, so it's probably not on the wall. Besides, he would have hidden it if it was a painting he didn't wish anyone to see – other than Flora and Luca."

We hunted around the studio, looking at canvases and frames stacked against the walls. My eyes kept drifting towards the desktop littered with artist tools: paintbrushes, oil paint tubes, paint scrapers, soiled rags, and a cheerful array of colourful palettes topped with mounds of blue, yellow, and red oil paints. Nothing had changed since last night, though the sheer quantity of items made it difficult to be certain.

Next to me, Ruby slid open the stuffed drawers of the large desk.

"I say, how would a framed canvas fit in a drawer?" asked Pixley.

"They might have cut it from the frame and rolled it up. Much easier to hide," said Ruby.

"Why all this fuss over this coal miner, anyway?" asked Pixley. "It seems like most people would rather forget they existed."

"True. And strikes are a dime a dozen in the Caribbean these days." I turned to Pixley. "What makes this strike so newsworthy?"

"Well, mining conditions are appalling. That's no surprise. But this newsreel I watched the other day made my blood boil."

Pixley's voice became a whisper. "The newsreel was called

'The Coal Girls', which made light of their situation. The announcer was chortling with glee when he said, 'Each girl carries a hundred pounds of coal in her basket, so they don't need any extra coal to keep them warm'."

Ruby crossed her arms. "And they probably said something offensive about dust and being 'dusky', didn't they?"

"Of course they did," said Pixley. "But to answer your original question, these strikes come at the same time as Italy's attack on Ethiopia."

"Ah, you mean it's all connected. Rising discontent across the globe," I said.

"Which makes large companies and governments nervous," said Ruby.

I scratched my head. "How does this relate to the painting?"

Ruby froze.

"What is it?" asked Pixley.

Ruby leaned over the desk, mumbling, "I wish I had a magnifying glass. Or a blasted monocle."

"Channelling Holmes or Lord Peter Wimsey," said Pixley.

"I could never fill their shoes," said Ruby.

"I'd much rather have tea with you than Sherlock or Wimsey," I said.

"Ever the loyal friend." But Ruby was still transfixed by the desk.

"Here, I'll look." I bent down. "There are bits of paint once you clear away this mess. Blue, yellow, and that blasted burnt umber following me around."

"Erm, it's not burnt umber," said Ruby.

Pixley poked his head between us. "You don't mean ..."

"Ruby is right," I sighed. "That splotch isn't brown paint. It's dried blood."

21

"Well, that tears it." Pixley rubbed his head. "The killer attacked Sir Montague in this studio. Unless there was a struggle and then he was killed downstairs."

"Seems unlikely given the lack of marks on his body," I said. "Other than the wound on his neck, we didn't see any cuts or obvious bruises."

Ruby stared at the sea. "Who benefits from Sir Montague's death? In terms of his will."

Pixley ran a finger across his mouth. "Daphne mentioned he was the last of the Dunbridges. Sir Montague never married, and had no siblings."

"He might have left his estate to a museum," I said.

"Sir Montague seems like the type to leave his estate to a living person or persons," said Ruby.

Pixley gave us a wry smile. "Helen is sweet on him."

"Mr Benbow told me as much," I said, "and he didn't like it."

"I expect Mr Benbow and Miss Poole inherit under his will. You've seen how he treated them like equals rather than servants," said Ruby.

"What about Flora? Or even Gwendolyn?" asked Pixley.

"Perhaps." That dreaded blotch on the desk stared back at me like a little angry rain cloud. "But wouldn't they receive smaller bequests? Nothing worth killing over."

"Unless they inherit a valuable painting," said Pixley.

"An excellent point, Mr Hayford," said Ruby. "Talking of which, I must ask Flora more about this forgery business."

Pixley gazed out of the French windows. "Such a lovely sunrise after such a nightmare. Perhaps Red and I ought to stroll the grounds to enjoy it whilst Ruby grills Flora."

We left Ruby to find Flora and donned nearly every piece of clothing we'd packed. Though the morning was calm, we both expected it to be cold. Swathed in coats, hats, and scarves, we waddled out the front door and into the morning sun.

Pixley pulled off his gloves. "Whew. It's rather warm, isn't it?" He unwound a thick woollen scarf and wrapped it around the neck of one of the serpents guarding the front door. Then he plopped his hat on the head of the other.

I shed one of my jackets and buttoned it around the serpent's torso, chuckling as I did so.

"Much improved," pronounced Pixley, tilting the flat cap askew on the serpent's head. "They are rather jolly now, and we need all the frivolity that's going."

"Good Lord, yes." I crooked my arm at an angle. "Shall we?"

"We shall." He hooked his arm into mine and then stopped. "Did you forget something?"

Pixley snapped his fingers. "My notebook. I'll just nip upstairs. I'll be back in a jiffy."

"Do you need it?"

"I'm a journalist, Red. A reporter without a notebook is like a chicken without feathers. I'll be back in two ticks."

I rambled towards the end of the drive, knowing that Pixley's "two ticks" would be closer to twenty minutes. When Pixley was working, he was early, but he was a bit more leisurely with everything else.

Admiring the early spring sea pink flowers and bluebells dotting the perimeter of the scrubby garden, I turned the corner of the house.

Charles Vane was sitting on a large rock with his own notebook in hand. I stepped backwards, wishing to avoid him. Then footsteps approached from the other direction.

Behind the low hedge, I watched a new scene unfold.

The footsteps belonged to Ruby, walking at a casual pace. The blue scarf knotted under her chin gave her an air of innocence.

Innocence, my foot. Ruby had calculated every step towards Charles.

"Oh, hello." Ruby eyed Charles. "Are you sketching?"

His pencil halted, and he squinted in the morning sun. "Sketching to calm my nerves after the horrors of last night."

"That's why I'm on a stroll. What are you sketching?"

He handed Ruby the notebook. She took a step backwards, her heels teetering on a rock. Quickly, she righted herself and shoved the book back into his hands.

"I say, is it that bad?" he asked.

"No, I'm just a little disconcerted. How did you capture my likeness so well? Especially since I wasn't sitting for you."

"Once seen, never forgotten."

With her eyes still on the sea, she asked, "Are you a secret painter, too? Is that why you were invited here?"

"No, my sketches are erratic at best," he said. "My father is the artist of the family. He's a painter in Barbados, and I've been selling his work in London through Luca's gallery. My parents aren't wealthy, or even comfortable, so the money his paintings fetch goes a long way."

"So the sugar company work is just a job?"

"Decidedly." He clicked open his leather cigarette case and offered it to Ruby.

She shook her head. "And you'd quit working for them if you could make enough money from your art?"

The silver smoke from Charles's cigarette ballooned, shifted, and waved in the wind.

"I say," said Charles, "when this is over, what about dinner in town? Go to a show, or even a public lecture, if that's your cup of tea?"

She gave a tiny snort. "The last worthwhile public lecture I attended was Marcus Garvey's speech at the Royal Albert Hall in 1928. My father took me, hoping it would make an impression. It certainly did."

Charles eyed her like a child admitting an act of gluttony involving a plate of biscuits. "I'm frightfully anti-intellectual. But I'm willing to learn. Who is this Marcus Garvey chap when he's at home?"

Someone tapped me on the shoulder, startling me. I slid off a large moss-covered rock and tumbled onto my backside. But I didn't stop there, somersaulting down the pebbled pathway. Only Pixley's firm hands prevented me from rolling down to the sea.

"Dash it, you scare like a newborn foal." Pixley helped me up, brushing dirt from my coat and removing twigs from my hair.

Now upright, I strolled with Pixley towards the jetty and recounted what I'd learned from my eavesdropping.

"Do you think John will return this morning?" I asked.

He kicked a pebble. "Haven't a clue. The story of his disappearance doesn't sit right."

I jabbed my finger at the empty jetty. "The boats have vanished!"

"So they have," said Pixley. "So we really are cut off. Even if John took one boat, there ought to be another."

"Won't the telephone be restored soon?"

"Not unless someone restores it, and I expect John's the only one who can do that."

"And Mr Tremore isn't due until Monday."

We stood in silence, listening to the waves lapping against the rocks. A cormorant gurgled and squawked in the distance.

"Come on, Red." Pixley turned and trotted along the cliff path. "No time for brooding. Let's assume that John Benbow is safely toddling around St Mary's. That still leaves this ghastly murder. Who did it?"

"It's rather obvious, but I'd plump for Charles Vane."

"Just because it's obvious doesn't mean it's wrong. Tell me why."

I dug my hands deeper into my pockets. "He's the fly in the oil paint – the only unknown and an imposter of sorts."

"But given his conversation with Ruby, his story makes more sense. And Ruby seems smitten by him," Pixley said.

Unconsciously mimicking Ruby, I tapped my teeth. "She certainly does, and she doesn't fall for anyone easily."

"Not like me," sighed Pixley. "Or even you, Red."

"Me?" My cheeks flamed with heat.

In a rare show of restraint, Pixley declined the opportunity to tease me further. "What about that conversation you overheard in the conservatory? If Charles is a spy, then it follows—"

"That Sir Montague was a spy?"

"It's plausible given what you said."

"Sir Montague was exhausted – as if he were tired of a game."

"Ah, an informant or unwilling spy. Not for money or the cause, but forced to do it," said Pixley

"What if Charles – or a sugar baron who employs him –

compelled Sir Montague to participate in their spying, and he finally rebelled?"

He rubbed his chin. "I see. And Charles killed him to stop him blowing the gaff on the whole charade."

"What about you? Who's at the top of Mr Hayford's list?"

Without hesitation, he said, "Dr Rafferty. Something shifty about that fellow."

"Oh?" I pulled my scarf tighter. "Not shifty. Perhaps mysterious. Or rude."

He gave me a quick, sidelong glance. "He's been perfectly convivial, but there's something else there, behind the eyes. Besides, I'd never trust a psycho-what's-it."

"Psychotherapist, Pix."

"My, you are a wee bit defensive, aren't you?"

"No, I just want to be accurate. And why do you suspect him? I mean, beyond him being secretive?"

"Well, being a big noise on Harley Street, he's probably up to his eyeballs in scandalous patient stories. You know the kind: Mrs Snooty-from-High-and-Mighty tells him everything about her politician husband's affairs. Imagine that happening every day, all day. The good doctor could be simply awash in cash by extorting his patients. Or selling information about his patients to others."

"That's unethical, Pix."

"So is murder, dear Red."

"Okay, let's say you're right: he's extorting his patients. Niall watches them painting their hearts out whilst they confess their sins with each brushstroke. How does murdering Sir Montague fit in?"

"Sir Montague discovers Dr Rafferty's little scheme, so Dr Rafferty silences him."

"We have absolutely no evidence of that. And how would Sir Montague find out?"

"Remember the invoice we found in Sir Montague's study? What if it wasn't for a regular patient appointment but was an excuse for Sir Montague to confront Dr Rafferty about his unethical behaviour?"

"It makes no sense. Why would Sir Montague allow Flora to invite him as a judge this weekend?"

As we crested a small hill, Luca's brown woollen cap came into view. He sat motionless on a bench, apparently contemplating St Mary's and the sea beyond.

"Should we talk to Luca? Find out more about last night?" I asked.

Pixley scratched his head. "Maybe just one of us ought to approach him. We don't want to make him defensive."

"Shall I?" I asked, hoping he'd dismiss the idea.

"No, not after he tried to push you into the sea." Pixley winked at me. "Besides, I'll talk to him, man to man."

"You are utterly hopeless sometimes, Pixley Hayford."

He gave me a little salute. "I aim to please. But seriously, I'll use my journalist skills to play the innocent outsider."

"Aye aye," I said. "I'll keep strolling. It will help me collect my thoughts, such as they are."

"Wait for me. It's unwise to wander the island with a murderer on the loose."

"If I stand here, Luca will become suspicious – I know I would."

"All right, then. I'll catch you up in a few minutes."

I pointed to the west. "I'll keep to that path towards the end of the island."

A gentle wind arose, and I buttoned up my jacket. The western side of the island was more exposed, so the wind grew stronger as I walked along the spongy earthen path.

Despite the horrors of last night, I marvelled at the raw beauty of the sea, the swooping, frantic seagulls, and a seal popping her head above the surface. She stared at me, snorted, and dipped back under the waves.

The narrow pathway meandered near the shingle beach before weaving inland, towards the pest house we'd seen on our arrival in Mr Tremore's boat. One wall had crumbled, and the white and grey stones lay in a haphazard pile overgrown with seagrass.

I poked my head through the front window, spotting a stone fireplace still holding a rusted pot on a chain. Moss and scrub had sprouted everywhere, lending colour to the white and grey walls. A wood frame on the wall held a scrap of embroidered stitchwork flapping in the breeze. A sharp pang of melancholy struck me as I imagined those enduring untold misfortune in this very house.

I scolded myself. *Mustn't be morbid, Fina.*

A light scraping noise came from within, a sound I soon dismissed as a mouse.

Near the crumbled wall, I spied something leaping inside and dashing towards the scraping noise. I thought it might be a weasel or stoat, but its orange fur told me otherwise.

"Tangerine!" I squealed. "What are you doing here? Your mother will be worried sick!"

I'd been right about the mouse. Tangerine made quick work of the poor thing, gulping it down in one go. He then moved on to capturing his dessert.

The kitten lay low, wiggling his hindquarters whilst his tail whipped side to side. His whiskers stood erect, and his eyes dilated. Tangerine's focus on his victim offered me a chance to scoop him up so I could return him to Flora.

One leg followed another as I ungracefully climbed through the window into the house, right behind Tangerine. Yet another grey mouse flitted across the rubble, splitting the cat's attention.

I must have been mimicking Tangerine, crouching down,

ready to spring on my prey. Carefully avoiding a wet patch of moss, I lifted one foot forward onto the debris, one step nearer to the cat. Then I became overconfident and moved the other foot forward quickly. My foot slipped.

As Tangerine flew out of the window, I toppled headlong onto the stones. Into a velvety darkness.

22

My face jerked as my brother tickled it with a fern. "Stop it, Connor!" I called.

With eyes suddenly open, I stared at the blue sky through the window. Still caught between the dream world and reality, I blinked, trying to clear my head.

Something danced across my hand.

"Bleh!" I cried, jolting upright. I brushed myself all over, ruffling my hair and throwing off my scarf. For good measure, I cried out once more in disgust and frustration. Finally, the skin-crawling sensation disappeared.

The sun from the window warmed my feet, restoring me to a shaky equilibrium. I craned my neck out of the window, looking up at the sky. From the sun's position, I guessed it must be early afternoon.

Rather cross with Pixley for abandoning me, I turned back towards the hall. I'd make him sorry for leaving me behind.

But first I tugged on my white scarf, stuck between the mossy stones.

Blast it.

I pulled at it again.

This time, the scarf came loose but also dislodged something else. It looked like a sun-bleached starfish. What business would such a creature have toddling up from the shore to this dratted house?

Curious. Did starfish sport black hair?

Perhaps it was a bit of seaweed or twigs.

I leaned over and inspected it more closely. My spine suddenly snapped back into its normal position.

That wasn't a starfish.

It was a very human hand.

A mouse ran over the hand, and I unleashed a guttural shriek. Like a blessed banshee. With complete and total abandon.

Now empty of screams, I flung myself over the window ledge and onto the soft earth outside. I dashed round the corner, crouching to keep myself from tripping and falling. As I turned another corner, I hit a wall, sending me reeling onto my backside. And into the mud.

"Miss Aubrey-Havelock! Fina!"

I stared at Niall's shoes squelching through the mud. He grabbed my waist and hauled me up. Though he wasn't tall, his arms were strong. Without another word, he began brushing off the caked dirt from my hands and sleeves.

Once he reached my hair, he stopped, letting his hand drop to his side. He had a gleam in his eye.

"Was that you? I heard a scream, so I came as quickly as I could."

Lips quivering, I just opened and closed my mouth. I must have used up my voice with those screams. The quivering soon gripped my entire body, and I simply couldn't stop.

"There," he said, taking off his jacket and draping it over me. "It's the shock. Whatever you spotted can wait. Let's get you back to the house. Your friend Ruby has been searching for you – I won't say she's frantic, but she is worried."

"I-I-I." At least I had managed one letter. That must be progress.

"No need to speak." He guided me up the path towards Serpentine Hall.

We walked in silence, and soon my body stopped shaking. Niall's hands still gripped my upper arms as we walked, having an inexplicably calming effect. I gave him a sidelong glance, but his eyes gazed ahead, giving away nothing about his busy brain.

"Yes, your friend has been searching for you," he said, picking up where he'd left off earlier. "She found bits of your clothing scattered about the drive, along with those of your friend Mr Hayford."

I pictured how the wind must have dislodged our clothes from the serpent statues guarding the house, tossing them to the ground. Ruby would be worried indeed, even if she knew we couldn't have gone very far.

"What happened to Pixley?" I said, trying to keep the alarm from my voice.

"He's also disappeared," said Niall.

"We must find him. He was speaking to Luca on the bench overlooking the jetty."

"I see." He stopped. I stole a look at his angular face, half-covered in shadow, and then turned away, pretending to brush the hair from my eyes.

He opened his mouth, but it was Ruby's voice that spoke.

"Feens! My goodness, Feens!" She dashed down the steep pathway from the side of the house. In an uncharacteristic show of affection, Miss Ruby Dove grabbed me in a boa-constrictor embrace, rocking me back and forth. Then she held me at arm's length, inspecting me from head to toe.

"I must be a sight." My voice still quavered.

"Never mind that. We'll warm you up with a proper cup of tea," said Ruby, sounding like her grandmother.

She looked back at Niall. "Thank you for finding her."

He'd become gruff again, shrugging off her words of thanks. "I'll find out what made her scream," he said.

"Pardon?" asked Ruby.

"Ah, right," said Niall. "You wouldn't have heard her scream from up here." A tiny smile played across his lips. "Though I must say Miss Aubrey-Havelock has quite the pair of lungs on her."

Inexplicably, I said, "My lungs are perfectly normal, I assure you."

Ruby looked at both of us and then coughed. "If you're going down there, Niall, you'd better not go alone."

"Ah, I can take care of myself," he said.

"Nevertheless," insisted Ruby, "let's not be foolish. There is a murderer about, after all." She eyed him speculatively, and I knew she'd stopped herself from saying, "Unless you're the murderer."

Niall rubbed his neck. "Now you mention it, it's probably wise to have a search party of sorts since Luca and Mr Hayford have disappeared as well."

"It's already sorted. Flora and Charles saw you two coming up the hill, so they went to fetch their coats and should join you soon. Gwendolyn has a headache, and Daphne is taking a nap. Helen is still asleep."

"Thank you, Miss Dove." Niall turned back. "You'll look after Fina now, won't you?"

23

Ruby handed me a cup of tea and two chocolate digestives. "My, my, Miss Aubrey-Havelock. What an admirer you have."

The biscuits proved more of a distraction than Ruby's words.

"Dear Feens," she continued, "has the lack of food sapped your brain completely?"

I chomped the second biscuit and washed it down with a swig of tea. Then I warmed my hands near the fire, shifting the mound of blankets on my knees and around my neck. "It happens. Now, what were you saying?"

She waved a hand. "It's not important. What's important is you're safe. And I expect they'll find Pixley soon."

"You don't think that Luca ..." I said, unable to finish the thought.

"Let's not fly off into wild flights of fancy. Believe me, my mind has already done that for the past few hours."

"You're right. Now, may I have another biscuit?" I felt like Oliver Twist with my ragged clothes.

Life brightened considerably as a plate of petits fours and chocolate sponges materialised in her hands. I bit into one of each. After all, I'd read in an advertisement that certain biscuits were "ideal for children's health". If they were good enough for the little blighters, they were good enough for me.

Feeling fortified, I tried to explain my movements. "I screamed because I discovered a hand. After I fell on the rubble and became unconscious for a few hours. I had been chasing Tangerine."

Ruby cocked her head. I imagined Niall must do the same when a patient said something perfectly barmy. "Chasing Tangerine. Rubble." She closed her eyes. "I can see that sequence, especially since Flora has been searching for her absentee cat."

"A hand."

"A hand. You say it so matter-of-factly."

"Well, that's all I saw," I said. "I certainly wasn't going to root around like some blasted truffle pig to discover if it was attached to a body. Not by a long chalk. Anyway, the short of it is that I screamed the house down. Quite literally, because a few stones fell from the wall."

"And you ran into Niall." Ruby suppressed a smile.

"Yes. Was he sent to find us?"

"No, not exactly."

"What? Pixley and I disappear, and you don't search for us?"

"Well, I assumed you were with Pixley and Luca. It was only recently I became very concerned."

"I see." I bit into a biscuit that disintegrated into my lap. Too tired to bother with appearances, I brushed the crumbs onto the floor. If they mixed in with the fireplace ash, they'd make the house smell pleasant.

"In any case, I expect the hand belongs to John Benbow, but we'll know that soon enough." I lowered my voice. "Before they all return to the house, tell me what Flora said to you when you questioned her."

"For someone who's usually so chatty, Flora was tight-lipped.

But she said Luca was involved in selling forgeries through his gallery. He's using the gallery as a conduit to sell to wealthy art collectors who think they're buying stolen paintings. However, they're not stolen – they're simply forgeries posing as stolen art."

"And the coal miner painting was just such a forgery? One that happened to be actually painted by Gwendolyn?" I surveyed my grubby fingers. "But how is it a forgery if Gwendolyn is the real painter? And why is Flora involved?"

Ruby rubbed her eyes. "I'll try to explain. In this case, 'forgery' means a range of dodgy practices. First, there's the side I already told you about: selling fake stolen art to credulous wealthy collectors. The other dodgy practice is this: Luca buys paintings by little-known artists for a mere pittance. Then he artificially increases their value by replacing the artist's signature with Sir Montague's."

"I see. It will make their value rocket because he's a famous painter."

"Precisely," said Ruby. "It's not conventional forgery, but it's unethical and possibly illegal."

I blinked. "So you take the best paintings from an artist who can't sell their paintings for high prices and then pass them off as the work of a famous artist. Where does Flora fit into this scheme?"

"She says she uncovered the plot because she knew the coal miner portrait was painted by Gwendolyn. Remember, Gwendolyn's paintings have remained rather obscure, so a Sir Montague signature would increase their value."

"But why was Flora discussing the painting with Luca and Sir Montague?"

"She says she was confronting them about it."

I snorted. "It didn't look that way."

Ruby held up her hands. "Flora says they begged her to keep quiet about it. They even offered her money."

"Which she says she didn't take."

Ruby laced her fingers together in her lap. "What do you mean 'she says'?"

"She is your friend, but you must admit the whole scenario is fishy."

Her voice rose. "Are you saying she's lying?"

"Who's lying?"

I turned and faced the new speaker.

Helen Poole stood in the doorway. Wrinkles of concern creased her ghostly white forehead, still half-covered by that lock of brown hair. And she looked as perplexed as I felt.

24

"What happened?" Helen held a hand to her head. "I feel like I've slept for days."

"In a manner of speaking, you have." Ruby rose from her chair. "Why don't you join us by the fire? We have plenty of tea and ..." She stared at my empty plate of biscuits.

"Thank you. I think I will." She poured herself a cup of tea and looked fixedly at me.

I held up a warning hand. "Before you ask, yes, I've been actually rolling around in the mud. Don't worry, I'll clean up my mess. Scout's honour."

"I see." She stirred her tea absently.

"Did you take too many sleeping pills?" asked Ruby.

"I didn't have enough analgesics, so I asked everyone if they had any to spare. Flora gave me tablets and so did Gwendolyn. Then Mr Vane, kind man that he is, gave me a full packet of a sleeping draught."

Ruby and I glanced at each other. Charles said Helen had rejected his offer.

With his tweed cap askew and tie loosened, Charles himself burst into the drawing room.

He goggled at Helen. "Hello. I'm glad you're alive."

His outburst shook me into a grim reality. I stared at Helen in horror: our own Rip Van Winkle. Whilst she'd been unconscious, Sir Montague had been murdered and John Benbow had disappeared. She had awoken to a completely altered world.

Charles eyed Ruby, and she gave him the tiniest of nods. The Y-shaped vein on Charles's forehead pulsed as his words came tumbling forth. "Ruby and Fina, it's most urgent that you come quickly. It, it has to do with Pixley. That's it. Pixley twisted his ankle and he's asking for you."

Though it was a rather dubious story, Helen was in no mental state to object.

"Right." Ruby put on her coat. "Feens, you'd better stay here in case Helen needs help. I expect she's weak still."

"Oh, I'll be fine," said Helen, "if you'd explain what happened whilst I was asleep."

Ruby's command for me to stay behind was a relief. I'd do anything to avoid the dreaded pest house. "Yes, of course," I said. "Perhaps Helen and I can make tea and sandwiches for everyone."

Helen rose. "The house feels empty, doesn't it? Where is everyone?"

Charles adjusted his cap. "Sorry, I forgot to tell you why Pixley twisted his ankle. Luca spotted a whale, and in the rush of everyone from the house to watch it, Pixley fell. But they're all still searching the horizon for the whale again. A rare sighting."

Whale indeed. Still, I supposed Charles's fibbing confirmed he was spy material.

Charles and Ruby hurried from the room.

After the front door closed, I clasped my hands together. "Right. I'll make sandwiches and tea. Would you like to join me or rest here?"

"Is there anyone else who'd like sandwiches?"

"Anyone else in the house?" I pondered. "I believe Gwendolyn and Daphne are lying down or asleep. One of them had a headache, apparently."

"Oh?" Helen looked at me, and again I realised she wouldn't understand. Then she stood up, drumming her fingers on the mantelpiece. "Strangely enough, I'm not particularly peckish. But I need your help with something. And then you can explain why everything seems topsy-turvy."

Always eager to please, I said, "Of course. And I could help you redress your bandage, though I must warn you I'm squeamish."

"I need your help with something else." She strode to the door, regaining her rapid, efficient step. "You're a person with a strong moral compass, and I have a rather, well, sticky ethical quandary." She twisted the door handle. "Come with me and I'll show you. It's too difficult to explain in the abstract."

We entered the ground floor hallway, and she led me into the study. Helen made a beeline for the bookshelf nearest the desk and pulled on a Shakespeare volume. The title was too small to read.

I stood in the doorway, scratching my head. Why would Helen Poole ask my opinion on the literary merit of a Shakespeare play?

Helen turned and winked. A creaking noise came from the wall, and the bookcase began to move. The door opened a few inches and stopped. Helen gave the bookcase a little shove, and it swung open into a darkened alcove.

She removed a pocket torch from behind the books and switched it on.

"Follow me," she said.

Secret rooms and passages had always fascinated me, even as a girl. My dearly departed brother had once discovered an old priest hole in a distant cousin's house, and we'd spent hours scampering in and out of it, frightening the maids. And though my imagination helped me maintain a healthy dose of scepticism and fear throughout the years, my curiosity usually won.

Helen shone her torch on a spiral staircase. "I want to show you something."

My mind urged me forward, but my body hesitated.

"Don't worry, I've cleared it of cobwebs." She laughed. It was a warm, reassuring laugh.

At the bottom of the staircase, the torchlight played about the room, lighting frames and canvases scattered about on the floor. Paintings leaned against each other like drunken revellers in the wee hours of the morning.

I gasped as Helen's torch lit on one particular canvas: the missing coal miner portrait.

"Are you surprised by all this?" asked Helen, taking my gasp as one of general astonishment rather than surprise at seeing the portrait. Her normally dulcet tones had become curiously neutral, and her face was unreadable in the darkness.

"Frankly, I am surprised." I added hastily, "By the secret passage and this secret room." What did Helen know about the forgery operation? She must know. She was Sir Montague's secretary. It was a significant point, but my addled brain struggled to understand why.

I was suddenly cold. Very cold indeed.

"So, what is your dilemma? How can I help you?" I asked casually, though my knees were shaking like jelly. Or like that ghastly custard Helen had served us yesterday.

Helen shone the torch on my face. "Tell me, Miss Aubrey-Havelock. What do you do with nosy parkers? Snitches? Gossips? People who thrive on others' misery?"

Shading my eyes with my hands, I gained a few seconds to think. Pixley's voice popped into my head. That was it – I would channel Pixley.

"I'm afraid you'll have to spell it out for me, Miss Poole. Helen. I'm woefully uninformed and all that." Well, it wasn't Pixley, but it was a start.

Helen snorted. "Forced insouciance isn't your line, Fina. Yours is the ingenuous little snoop. That's what you are: a snoop."

I tapped my foot. "It's difficult to think when you're blinding me."

"Of course. I'll move the light."

In a flash, Helen dropped the torch and leapt forward with her uninjured hand balled into a fist. In one swift motion, the cursed woman punched me in the gut. Right in my stomach.

I doubled over and fell onto the floor from the searing pain and shock. After a few seconds, I lifted my head from the floor in a rage. I might not have been so angry if she had socked me in the jaw; it was the literal and figurative below-the-belt assault that made me see red. With the pain still shooting through my stomach, I lifted myself on one hand, trying to scramble to my feet.

Helen was already halfway up the stairs when I finally rose. Still propelled by anger, my legs flew up the steps, hoping I might catch her up. If I grabbed onto her frock, I could yank her downwards.

In one last desperate attempt, my arm shot out, just brushing the hem of her skirt. I teetered for a moment, staring into the darkness. Then I lost my balance and collapsed onto the stairs.

Pixley would have said, "Hard lines, Red."

As I lay in a pathetic heap, Helen's evil chuckle from above sent the hairs prickling on my arms. The room spun, but I still heard the upstairs door creak shut, cutting off the weak light filtering downstairs.

And as Pixley would have said, I was well and truly in the soup.

My few moments of terror in the complete darkness soon gave way to a spiralling self-pity and despair. No one would ever find me. Helen would say I'd fallen over a cliff. Or maybe that I was the murderer and had thrown myself into the sea in a fit of remorse.

Steady on, Fina. Pull yourself together.

The best plan was to pretend that Ruby and Pixley were trapped in this room too. We would be roaming around together, trying to find a way out.

I closed my eyes, recalling various objects in the room. Paintings were propped up against the wall. The room had to be near the kitchen or the larder. I shivered. Or even the billiard room where they'd moved Sir Montague's body.

Don't be morbid, Fina. Closing my eyes again, I remembered absently rifling through a stack of paintings against the wall. What was so significant about them?

That was it! I scrambled to my feet. My fingers found the bannister on the staircase. I retraced my steps from the moment I'd descended the stairs. Leaning down, my hands brushed against a frame. The texture was wrong, so I groped about for another nearby frame. Bingo!

I'd found a very smooth frame and lifted it back from the wall.

A beam of golden light burst through a tiny hole where the wall met the floor. I squatted and – probably unwisely – stuck my finger into what I decided must be a mousehole. Clearly, I'd unfairly damned the mice of Cutmere Perch, even given our dreadful encounter in the pest house.

Even if Helen returned, I relished my victory – at least I had a little light to contemplate my last moments on earth. I gulped and shook my head like a wet cat, pushing away these unprofitable thoughts.

Using what light there was, I began shoving paintings to the side. Perhaps the wall held more mouseholes? Sure enough, another little archway popped up. Soon, it became a sort of game. In a frenzy, I cleared all the paintings away from the wall. Like dominoes, the last stack had fallen over. The light of my third mousehole illuminated a tiny envelope falling from a frame. I scooped it up.

"Ow!" I cried, looking down at the floor. My finger had brushed a razor blade underneath the envelope.

As I sucked on my finger, a rattling noise shook the stairs above. Perhaps Ruby and Pixley were rattling the bookcase shelf. They'd come to rescue me!

I yelled, and the rattling increased. I yelled again.

The rattling halted.

My nerves were shot to pieces, and to make matters worse, I realised it might be foolhardy to make noise. Gwendolyn or Daphne could wake up, and Helen might try to silence them as well. Or hurry about silencing me.

A loud bang interrupted my thoughts. Quick footsteps followed – a scurrying footstep. A little burst of joy burbled up from inside me.

It couldn't be Helen's footstep – she'd never scurry, even if she were running. Her pace would be simply accelerated like a swan on a pond.

Then everything clicked into place. Before the scurrier arrived, I knew who it was.

25

"Gwendolyn!" I cried. "I never thought I'd be—"

"Glad to see me?" A weak light filtered in from upstairs, making Gwendolyn's squinting eyes just visible through her spectacles.

For a moment, I shrunk back. Perhaps this was yet another ruse. Perhaps Helen and Gwendolyn were in it together.

"I've taken Helen's keys and locked her in her room," Gwendolyn held out her small hand. "Let's go upstairs, shall we?"

Her eyes scanned the room with something akin to grim pleasure – that strange satisfaction at being proven correct about an impending tragedy, such as predicting the sinking of an ocean liner.

Needing no encouragement to leave my mice friends behind, I leapt up the stairs, two at a time.

"No need to hurry," said Gwendolyn. "As I said, I locked Helen in her room."

"How did you find me? And why did you lock her in?"

"Her star turn as Sleeping Beauty was never convincing. Perhaps it's because I have a naturally suspicious mind. Or, like you, I observe things. At first, her disappearance into slumberland made perfect sense, but when Sir Montague was murdered, I began to suspect her. So I bided my time, waiting, until I realised that sooner or later she'd have to wake up. If she were the murderer, her curiosity would simply get the better of her."

"When almost everyone left the house, you stayed behind."

"Yes. I concealed myself in your room, since it was next to Helen's. Then I waited. I followed her downstairs and then hid in the studio across from the study. When she exited the study again, I asked her for her keys."

"And she gave them to you?"

"She believed my story that I needed coal for my fireplace. She offered to fetch it – even with her injured arm – but I said she should rest after her ordeal. Once she handed over the keys, I simply locked her in her bedroom after she closed the door."

"Couldn't the others hear her yelling?"

"The walls of Serpentine Hall are marvellously thick. In any case, I apologise for how long it took to rescue you – I couldn't locate the right books to pull for the secret passage."

"It was Shakespeare, right?"

"Yes. *Macbeth*."

I shivered. "Selkies and kelpies. Helen does remind me of Lady Macbeth."

We were now in the study. I heaved the heavy bookshelf door closed and followed Gwendolyn.

"Fina, I—"

But Gwendolyn's words were cut short.

A pair of gloved hands swung a shining white vase above her head. The hands brought it down on her in a shower of splintering porcelain. She swayed and fell into a crumpled heap on the floor.

A FAMILIAR STOCKY figure stepped from behind the study door.

"Pixley!" I cried, first in surprise and then in horror.

"Red! Are you all right?" He rushed forward, trailed by a rumpled Luca.

I drew back from Pixley's embrace.

He surveyed me. "What the devil?"

"What have you done? Why did you hit her? Why were you waiting for her?"

Luca came forward, running his hand through his spiky hair. "Fina, I can explain."

"Quiet!" With maximum effort, I regained my composure. What was left of it, anyway. In a softer voice, I said, "Let's hear what Pixley has to say."

Daphne materialised in the doorway, rubbing her eyes. "Darlings, why all the racket? I—" She bent over Gwendolyn's body, sprawled like a snow angel on the floor.

"Gwendolyn? What's happened to Gwendolyn?"

More footsteps. Running. Soon, the study was enveloped in a crowd of people fawning over Gwendolyn. Of course, everyone had different ideas about how to proceed.

But my only concern was Pixley and his inexplicable behaviour. I grabbed his arm and yanked him into a corner.

Ruby rushed forward out of the crowd. "What happened, Feens? We heard a terrible smashing sound and came running from outside."

She looked me up and down. "You have blood on your frock!"

Blood had dribbled down my front. "Oh, it's nothing. I cut myself on a razor in that blasted secret room."

Daphne and Niall lifted Gwendolyn and carried her out of the study. Soon the room was blessedly clear of other people, including Luca, who I'd shooed away.

I levelled my gaze at Pixley.

"Feens, why are you staring at Pix like that?"

"He was about to explain why, weren't you, Pix?"

He puffed out his cheeks. "It's like this. Luca and I had quite a chinwag on that bench. He has vast stores of information about Ethiopia, since his father had been a general in the Italian army. So we started arguing ... arguing isn't the right word – debating is more accurate. He is a most amazing chap. We became completely lost in discussion."

"Most intriguing," said Ruby drily.

Matching Ruby's sarcasm, I said, "Whilst I was knocked out cold with mice running all over me. Next to a dead body."

"I'm really sorry, Red. You had disappeared, so I assumed you'd toddled back to the house." He squeezed his cap in his hands. "It was a reasonable assumption. After all, I'd never have expected you to be in the pest house. It wasn't like you to step inside such an eerie place."

"Flora's cat was in there, so I was trying to catch it."

"Which we just did," Ruby put in.

"Anyway," said Pixley, "Luca and I walked back and forth around the island, until we finally returned to discussing the murder."

"Took you long enough." Was Pixley infatuated with Luca?

Pixley threw up his hands. "Don't blame me! I was trying to lull Luca into a sense of security. It's something we journalists do, you know."

I held my tongue. Regardless of the reason for Pixley's inordinate focus on Luca, I ought to hear his explanation.

"Gradually, Luca told me more about Gwendolyn, and how he suspected her of carrying a grudge against Sir Montague – a fact borne out by her general state of paranoia about this weekend. If she thought he was masterminding a scheme against her, she might 'snap' and kill him."

"If that's true," said Ruby, "then she must have also killed

John Benbow." She put a hand on my arm. "The hand you found, Feens, was indeed part of Mr Benbow's body. He was hit on the back of the head. There's no way to tell who did it, though. Any one of us could have lured him down there, and we don't know when he died."

My lips tingled and my eyes welled. I had sensed all along it had been John, and yet this confirmation brought on a wave of depression. A wave soon replaced with a wave of another emotion. Anger. Fury.

I turned on Pixley. "I still don't see how your cosy chat with Luca prompted you to cosh Gwendolyn."

"Sorry," he said, shamefaced. "But I was coming to that. Luca and I returned to the Hall and no one was about. The only person we saw was Gwendolyn, though she hadn't spotted us. We followed her, staying back just as she entered the study. I peeked around the corner and watched her heading down a secret passage! Then I heard the two of you and, well, I assumed the worst, especially since Luca had already convinced me Gwendolyn had done it."

I had to look away from his stare.

"You must believe me, Red. I wanted to protect you and collar the murderer."

My shoulders drooped. "I believe you." Then my brain cleared. "Gwendolyn said she locked Helen in her bedroom. Should we make sure she's really locked in? After all, she's the murderer."

Ruby tapped her teeth. "We must find Helen. Urgently."

26

Helen had simply vanished from the island. As Gwendolyn recovered from Pixley's porcelain assault, the remaining guests roamed about the house and grounds, searching for Helen in the dwindling light. Pixley and Ruby even searched the secret room with the paintings, as I had little desire to return. I'd told them about the coal miner painting also hidden away there, but it, too, had vanished.

Whilst everyone floated about with restless energy, our trio found ourselves in John Benbow's room. I thought we'd wandered in by accident, but I should have known better; Ruby pounced on the papers we'd seen on his desk.

She pressed a forefinger on the paper, groaning. "I'll swear this stack of papers was thicker the last time we saw it."

"And tidier," said Pixley. "Someone without Mr Benbow's organisational abilities tried to square the paper stack."

"What's missing?" I asked.

She tapped her teeth. "I have a hunch it's the will."

"Let's assume Helen and John benefited from this missing will," I said. "But as John is dead and Helen has …"

"Toddled off to heaven?" asked Pixley.

"It's plausible," I said, though she might be headed for warmer underworld climes.

"If both John and Helen have died," said Ruby, "then someone else must benefit from Sir Montague's will."

Pixley rubbed both hands over his eyes. "Even if I'd managed forty winks last night, I'd still be lost."

Ruby opened a leather satchel she'd been carrying under her arm. "Never fear, Mr Hayford. I took the liberty of borrowing Sir Montague's paints." She withdrew several paint tubes and lined them up on the bed.

Pixley and I shot a glance at each other.

"I say, it's a smashing time for an art tutorial. Or have you become Dr Rafferty's patient, ready to paint your childhood?" He winked at me. "I thought his newest patient would be dear Red."

I kicked Pixley's foot.

"Ow!"

"Serves you right, you beast."

Ruby ignored our antics and held up a tube of Burnt Umber.

I scowled at the crumpled brown tube.

"Let's play a game," said Ruby. "Remember Mr Benbow saying how much Sir Montague loved parlour games?"

"Go on," said Pixley.

"Let's see what we can learn from each colour at Serpentine Hall."

Pixley rubbed his hands. "I'm game. Let's start with my favourite."

Ruby held up a wrinkled tube of Zinc White.

"Bingo! How'd you know Charles is my number-one suspect?"

"I'm familiar with your methods, Watson."

Pixley flounced his jacket and stuck his hands behind his

back, pacing the room like a wandering pheasant. "'Pluralitas non est ponenda sine necessitate.' Whilst Charles Vane is, in many ways, the most obvious suspect, Occam's Razor applies."

"Do tell, Professor Hayford," I said. "I never remember principles."

"Occam's Razor means the simplest answer is often the truth. Charles Vane is here under false pretences, working for dubious sugar concerns in the Caribbean. Sir Montague was involved – either with the sugar companies or spying on behalf of Her Majesty's Government. However, Sir Montague no longer wants to play this spying game. He picks up his proverbial marbles to go home, but Charles is threatened by this. So, Sir Montague had to travel to the pearly gates. What's more, Zinc White is like a blank slate: that's what Charles Vane is. An unknown quantity."

Ruby's eyes dropped to the floor, avoiding the truth of Pixley's words. Whether Ruby had fallen for Charles because he resembled Ian or had some other attractive quality, I did not know. But she was definitely infatuated.

But pursuing the matter would only make her defensive, so I continued the paint-tube game.

I held up the tightly rolled tube of Perylene Black. "I plump for the mysterious Perylene Black. An iridescent colour that—"

"You'd make a spiffing auctioneer at Sotheby's," said Pixley.

"What Feens says is significant," said Ruby. "Black is the colour of introspection, and perylene's iridescence is even more mysterious."

"You mean there's more to Gwendolyn than meets the eye," said Pixley.

"Meaning she's the murderer, of course," I said.

"You would say that," Pixley chuckled, "after she asked you to pose sans your knickers."

"Don't be crude, Pix. It's true I hold a grudge against her, but that's exactly why I suspect her. She holds grudges. Colossal grudges."

"On display at the Finch Gallery." Ruby flipped the tube between her fingers. "Gwendolyn's chip on her shoulder is monumental, and this contest might have pushed her over the edge. Hence the vicious attack on Sir Montague."

"She's absolutely gaga. Bonkers," I said.

"And I thought I had a way with words," said Pixley. "But let's hear Ruby's favourite horse in this race."

Without hesitation, she pounced on Burgundy and Turner's Yellow.

"I'll be a rabbit's cousin," breathed Pixley. "Accomplices. Co-conspirators. The old one-two punch, the—"

"Yes, thank you, Pix." Ruby held the yellow to her cheek. "Remember how I heard a man laughing along with Daphne in her room?"

I gulped. "It was Niall."

"Well, she was all over him like a rash, wasn't she? Saying how he was 'heaven on a stick'," said Pixley in a falsetto.

"Correct words, but not a proper impression," I said.

"Ah, as I suspected, Red's name is ever the right choice." Pixley pointed at my cheeks. I knew full well they were scarlet from the warmth creeping up my neck.

"Stop teasing her, Pix. After all, I've seen how he looks at her—"

I stamped my foot, determined to ignore Pixley's provocation. "Why would they kill Sir Montague? How would either of them benefit?"

Instead of answering, Ruby put a finger to her mouth and crept towards the door. She flung it open, and Luca tumbled into the room.

Ruby said nothing, merely opening her palm in an inquiring gesture.

He scrambled to his feet. "I-I-I heard voices coming from Mr Benbow's room, and quite naturally thought it peculiar since he's, well ..."

"No longer with us?" Pixley put in. "Perfectly natural under the circs."

I was dubious. "Couldn't you hear our voices? Why not simply tap on the door?"

Luca ran his fingers through his hedgehog hair. "I'm afraid I'm not myself. The murders and lack of sleep have all conspired to—"

Ruby held out her hand. "Come in and tell us all about your painting business, Luca."

"Your real painting business," I said.

Luca took one tentative step towards us. "My real painting business?"

"The business of forgeries, or near forgeries," said Ruby quietly.

Luca goggled at Ruby. "Forgery? Surely not. It's common enough in the gallery business, but I've never dabbled."

"Never?" asked Pixley, just as gently as Ruby.

Luca crossed his arms. "Never."

I stepped towards Luca, my heart thumping. "What about your cosy chat with Sir Montague and Flora just before he was murdered?"

Luca's eyes darted around the room. Like a rodent caught in a trap, even his nose twitched in alarm.

Ruby put her hand in her pocket and withdrew the photograph of the coal miner painting. "If you deny Fina's claim, there's always this."

Luca gulped.

"And Southampton," she added.

I wondered what Southampton had to do with it.

But Luca hung his head. "It's not what you think. I promise you, it's not what you think."

And then a shot rang out from deep within Serpentine Hall.

27

"Did you hear that?" Flora dashed down the hall, her long white skirt swishing and glowing in the darkness.

"It came from below stairs," called Luca. His wiry frame far outpaced any of us.

Niall joined us on the landing, his hair more dishevelled than ever. "Where's Daphne?"

Even in that moment of terror, disappointment jabbed my stomach. Why fixate on Daphne?

In a comic scene under any other circumstances, we hurried downstairs in a cluster, forming a bottleneck that nearly sent me flying over the bannister.

We finally arrived below stairs. Ruby hurried into the kitchen, turning and shaking her head. Flora did the same with the larder. Daphne and Luca bounded towards the billiard room.

Luca jiggled the handle. "Damn and blast it! It's locked."

Niall pointed to a long bench lining one wall. "Let's use this as a battering ram."

We all gripped the bench and rammed it against the door.

But it was so long we couldn't gain enough momentum without hitting the opposite wall.

"I'll be back in a moment." Without waiting for a response, Niall dashed up the stairs.

Charles flew past him down the stairs in his white dressing gown. "What happened? I was in the bath."

"Who has a key?" asked Flora. "There must be a key."

Everyone shook their heads.

"Where's Gwendolyn?" I asked. "She took Helen's keys."

"She did receive a terrific wallop on the head, remember? She's resting upstairs."

Kicking off her shoes, Ruby hurtled towards the stairs. She called back, "I have keys in my room!"

We all stared at the door, willing it to open.

"We can't just stand here," wheezed Luca. He slid up and down the wall as if he were having a fit. With one great heave, his whole body slumped to the floor.

Pixley and I knelt down near Luca, lifting his feet and cradling his head. His eyes remained shut but flickered once or twice.

Niall reappeared with a screwdriver, and I waved him away from Luca, urging him to pry open the door.

He obeyed, jamming the tool into the door.

Following a loud splintering noise, it finally creaked open on its hinges.

"Well done, Niall," Charles whispered.

A rush of footsteps was followed by gasps and cries.

"Helen!" called Flora in an urgent tone. One of willing someone awake.

As if in response, Luca's eyes popped open, and he leapt up from the floor. He pushed past everyone and fell to his knees near Helen's sprawled body.

A dark pool of blood had ballooned near her head, right

next to a revolver. Though she lay on her stomach, her head turned to the side. Her one eye was covered by that lock of hair, just as it had covered her in life.

Luca buried his face in her jumper. "No, Helen. No, no, no."

"Come, Luca," whispered Flora.

Pixley put a hand on Luca's shoulder. "Come now, old man. She can't be helped anymore."

I stood still, consumed by Luca's affection for Helen. Were they lovers? Surely they knew each other before this weekend, but were they romantically involved?

Just as Ruby rushed in, jingling her keys, Flora marched over to one of the billiard tables and yanked off the dust cover. Then she marched back and draped the cover over Helen's body, partially covering Luca as well.

"Flora, give the man a moment," said Niall quietly.

She jerked her head towards Niall, blinking. But she held up the cover in mid-air as if she were making a bed. Luca rose and stumbled towards the door.

With her mouth set in a grim line, she let the drape float over Helen's body. Then she turned towards the huddled crowd in the doorway. "I don't know about you, but I need a drink."

A warming brandy was exactly what I needed. But if her tight grip on my arm was any indication, Ruby had other plans.

Everyone fled from the grisly scene, leaving our trio with the two bodies. The room had become a cemetery.

Ruby rattled the handle on the broken door. "The door was locked from the outside since Gwendolyn has the other keys."

"What about your keys – the ones we took from John's room?" asked Pixley. "Could someone have taken them from your room and then returned them without you noticing?"

"Not possible," said Ruby. "I put a tiny piece of paper on the drawer where I hid them. If anyone had opened it, that piece of paper would have flown away."

"Fortunately, you haven't left our sight," I said. "Otherwise, you'd be suspect number two – after Gwendolyn, of course."

"Well, what are we waiting for? Let's find Gwendolyn and ask her about the keys." Pixley moved towards the door and then stopped. "Wait. If Helen were locked in the billiard room whilst we were searching for her, why didn't we find her?"

"I expect the billiard room is the one place no one would have searched. My guess is everyone avoided this floor altogether since it also has the larder."

"Still," he said, "wouldn't we have heard her yelling?"

Murmuring to herself, Ruby ran her shoe over the floor in a little circle, making a soft, grating noise.

"Ah, Ruby. What are you doing?" asked Pixley.

A white powder covered the tip of her shoe.

"Is that sand?" I asked.

"Great Scott!" cried Pixley. "It's not cocaine, is it?"

Ruby chuckled. "Quite the imagination, Pix. No, I think it's something more mundane. Follow me."

"Oh no." I stamped a foot. "We're not going in there."

"Just for a moment, I promise. Then you can have your brandy," she said.

Pixley also hesitated. "I still don't understand why we're not waking the sleeping beauty upstairs, also known as Gwendolyn Brice. She must be the murderer."

"Wouldn't it be a bit obvious?" asked Ruby.

"Could be a double-bluff," said Pixley.

"Possibly," said Ruby. "Though with that bump on her head, it seems unlikely. Which leaves just me as prime suspect."

"We'd witness that you never left our sides," I said.

"I'm not sure the police would believe you," she said.

Pixley smashed his fist into his hand. "Ruby's right. We also might be tried as co-conspirators."

That was enough motivation for me to follow Ruby's intuition. Into the larder, where everything had changed.

"Selkies and kelpies!" The white powder we'd seen in the billiard room blanketed the floor.

"It's flour." Ruby sat on her haunches, scanning the torn remains of a burst sack. She held up the fabric to the light, revealing a round hole in the material.

As Pixley and I stared at it, Ruby fell to her knees and plunged her hands into the piles of loose flour scattered about.

"Erm, Ruby," said Pixley in a soothing voice. "As amusing as that looks, it's not the time to frolic in a sandpit. Or flourpit, rather."

Ignoring him, she puffed clouds of flour about, creating a thick fog of white that soon coated everything, including me and Pixley.

"Bingo!" The ghostlike figure of Ruby popped up, holding something small between her fingers.

"It's a bullet!" I paused. "Helen was shot in here?"

Ruby spat flour from her mouth. "Not quite, Feens. But almost. I was completely wrong before, but now it all makes sense."

"I say, are you all right in here?" Charles appeared, coughing and waving away clouds of flour.

Quickly, Ruby hid the bullet behind her back. "Just experimenting with something. Has something else happened?"

He rubbed his forehead. "Daphne's missing. We cannot find her anywhere."

28

The warm glow of brandy spread from my neck down to my toes. The crackling fire and ticking clock almost made this an enjoyable scene. But I couldn't escape the worried faces dotted around the drawing room.

An early evening wind was rising, blotting out the relative calm of the day. Raindrops speckled the windowpanes, interrupted only by an occasional tree branch scraping the window.

Pixley lifted his snifter towards the window. "If Daphne were wandering the island, this weather would bring her scampering home. She wouldn't fancy damaging her beautiful clothes, and nor would I."

Gwendolyn snorted. "Can't you see? She's dead. D-e-a-d."

Despite Gwendolyn's unique form of bravado, her voice quavered and her hands shook.

Sleeping Beauty, as Pixley had named Gwendolyn, had finally arisen. Niall said it would have been nearly impossible for Gwendolyn to murder Helen, even if she'd been seen roaming about the house. That had let Gwendolyn off the hook. And fortunately for our trio, everyone found Ruby's explanation of her hidden keys convincing. Besides, Ruby's whereabouts had been witnessed by multiple people the entire afternoon.

Luca glared at Gwendolyn. Suddenly, he hurled his brandy glass into the fire. The flames lapped up the brandy, growing and roaring, then subsiding into their normal size.

So Luca did have a temper. That calm, cool, and collected manner was probably genuine, but woe betide anyone who crossed him.

He pointed a long white finger at Gwendolyn. "You're the reason we're all here on this godforsaken island! If you'd left well enough alone, Helen would still be alive."

Ever the journalist, Pixley stepped in. "Helen Poole meant a great deal to you, didn't she?"

Luca blinked his red eyes and hurried from the room.

"Well, then." Pixley set down his brandy glass. "I managed to muck that up."

"Does anyone know why Luca is so distraught?" Ruby scanned the room. "Were Luca and Helen lovers?"

Niall stretched his legs towards the fire. "It will all come out once the police arrive, so I'll tell you. Helen visited my office a few times, though she wasn't an official patient."

Charles crossed his arms. "What was she, then?"

Niall's eyes fixed on a fox figurine perched on the window. "She was Luca's sister. His half-sister, to be precise."

Despite our exhaustion, the room filled with excited chatter.

Ruby silenced it by raising her finger. "Did they have the same mother or father?"

"Same father." Niall turned his seat to face us all. "Luca's father was named Marco Gatti."

"I may be daft, but why isn't Helen's last name also Gatti?" I asked.

Niall flicked an invisible bit of dust from his trousers. "I'd never call you daft, Fina. Marco Gatti had an affair with Lucinda

Poole, a minor member of the aristocracy. Luca's mother – Marco's wife – had died, and Lucinda Poole was unmarried. There was a scandal, but no one knew there was a baby."

"So Helen's cut-glass accent was real," said Pixley.

"Indeed. Helen was raised as Lucinda's niece. The story was that her parents died in a motorcar accident. When Helen came of age, they told her who she really was. Within a few months of this news, Lucinda fell ill and died. Unfortunately for Helen, this also coincided with some ill-timed investments made by Lucinda's older brother. The family became destitute overnight."

Charles blinked. "So Helen became Sir Montague's housekeeper and secretary."

"After a series of other such positions" – Niall wrinkled his brow – "none of which improved poor Helen's cookery skills."

Gwendolyn clicked her tongue. "I cannot understand it. We have three bodies, and possibly a fourth, all killed in different ways."

"And with no particular, obvious reason," Flora put in. "It must be a madman wandering the island. He must have lived in a cave here for years, eating seaweed and fish." I'd seen that fire in her eyes on the first day. "Then, when he can no longer take it, he comes in here and kills Sir Montague. He wants to be lord of the manor, or whatever you Brits call it."

Pixley's eyes were alight too, though his signalled amusement. He loved a good story, even if it was fiction. "Go on. And then?"

The fire died in Flora's eyes and she covered her face. "It's just so awful. Horrible."

Ruby licked her lips, biding her time to speak. "I'm afraid it's simply untrue, Flora. It has to be one of us."

"Miss Dove's right," sighed Niall. "It must be one of us."

Gwendolyn rose and touched her hair. "Well, we'll gain nothing by unprofitable speculation. When the police arrive, they'll sort it out. In the meantime, I'm going to take a steaming hot bath."

I eyed Gwendolyn. Surely someone so unaffected must be barmy. Barmy enough to be the murderer.

"You'd better barricade the door to the bath, Gwendolyn," said Charles. "We've had a stabbing, a bludgeoning, and a shooting. Let's not add drowning to the list."

"Unless that's what's already happened to Daphne," I blurted.

Everyone's eyes turned to me.

Ruby came to my defence. "It's possible." She pointed towards the rain-spattered window. "Has anyone searched her room?"

Niall held up a finger. "I looked in briefly. Nothing was out of place."

Pixley slapped his legs. "Well, what are we waiting for?"

～

MY EYES WERE starchy and my mouth was raw. I had complete confidence in Ruby, but I hoped her grey cells would spark to life soon.

Daphne's yellow room had that sour odour that comes from having all the windows closed. The vase of daffodils drooped over her travelling typewriter on a small golden desk. Next to the typewriter sat a bowl of withered though persistently cheerful lemons.

Instead of joining in the search, I observed the others, hoping it might spark my little grey cells, if not Ruby's.

Ruby made perfunctory movements, opening and slamming drawers, whilst Pixley threw himself into the task, sending papers flying everywhere.

Charles sorted through a stack of books ranging from Freud

to Flaubert. He flipped through each one, shaking it and then setting it down.

Flora flitted from desk to bed to wardrobe with no apparent purpose, though her eyes remained sharp and watchful.

Niall fixated on Daphne's writing desk. He opened one drawer, frowned, closed it, and opened another. Then he moved in front of the desk, where I couldn't monitor his movements. But I heard the distinct whirring a typewriter makes when one removes a piece of paper.

Ruby stepped forward. "Was there anything important in the typewriter, Niall?"

His head jerked up. "What? Oh, no. Just tidying it." He crumpled the paper and stuffed it into his pocket.

"What are you expecting to find, Ruby?" asked Charles.

She puffed her cheeks and blew them out. "Anything to clear up this nightmare."

My eyes remained fixed on Niall's jacket pocket. If I could only slip my hand in whilst he was distracted ...

Pixley piloted me towards a corner and whispered, "Why don't you distract your boyfriend whilst I pick his pocket?"

"My—" I exclaimed indignantly.

All heads in the room swivelled towards me.

"My shoe is untied!" I yelped.

Pixley raised his eyes to the heavens.

Niall approached us. "Miss Aubrey-Havelock, we ought to make an appointment for you at my practice."

"Why?"

He smirked and pointed at my feet. "You don't have any shoelaces."

Distracted by Pixley's hand reaching into Niall's pocket, I burbled, "I forgot I put on a new pair."

Suddenly, Niall spun round and grabbed Pixley's wrist.

"Don't they teach journalists ethics these days, Mr Hayford? One must not steal for a scoop."

"You're hurting me," was all Pixley said, letting the crumpled paper fall to the floor.

Niall's tensed body relaxed, letting go of Pixley's wrist.

Charles slipped in between us and snatched the paper. "Let's see what you've been up to, Dr Freud."

Shaking his head and the paper, Charles handed the wrinkled sheet to Ruby. "It's blank."

"What else did you expect?" asked Niall, his voice rising in a taunting tone.

Ruby smoothed the paper and then her hair. "It's blank," she repeated absently.

Pixley brushed his hands together in a cleansing motion. "I suggest we adjourn to the drawing room and have a tipple. A whisky will restore my mind to a blank slate. For better or for worse."

"Blank, blank paper, blank slate. Oui," said Ruby.

She grabbed Pixley's face with both hands and planted a kiss on his forehead. "Oh, the wondrous Hayford has returned. You've done it, my friend, you've done it."

29

Ruby jabbed the poker at the dying fire. "I've let myself be led astray."

A sharp gust of wind banged against the windows, making us all jump. Surely Daphne couldn't be out in this weather. Unless she was the murderer. Or she had been murdered herself.

"All this suspense is putting me on edge." Luca slumped in a wingback chair, a shadow of his former self. With glassy pinprick eyes, his sallow face stared into the fire.

"You seem perfectly relaxed to me," said Flora.

"Because Luca takes drugs, of course," said Ruby.

Pixley slapped his knee. "So that was it. Heroin. I ought to have known."

"Quite right, Mr Hayford," said Niall. "I ought to have noticed the classic signs. But I've been rather distracted."

Luca tried and failed to sit upright in his chair, sending his teacup rolling to the floor. His chin rested on his chest, and he closed his eyes. Soon, a soft snore filled the room.

Flora shook him. "Luca, wake up. Wake up!" she said with increasing ferocity.

"It's all right, Flora," said Ruby. "Let him sleep. We'll wake him when we need him."

I blew into my fringe. "I'm too exhausted to make my question diplomatic, so here it is: did Luca push me into the water because of his drugs habit? And is he the murderer?"

Flora goggled at me. "Luca pushed you into the water? Are you sure?"

"You do have a rather vivid imagination, Miss Aubrey-Havelock," Charles chipped in.

Pressing my hands against the soft arms of the chair, I rose in my seat. "What would you know about it?"

"I heard about your antics at Luca's gallery opening. You thought Gwendolyn Brice had a bomb that was actually a black candle."

"Look here," said Pixley, also rising from his seat.

Ruby opened her mouth, but Niall's voice rang out. "Miss Aubrey-Havelock has an admirably fulsome imagination, one that does her credit. And I can confirm her story. Luca did indeed push her into the water."

"Why didn't you say something?" I asked.

"To be honest, I thought it was my own imagination playing up. But if you saw it, then we can't both be wrong."

"Fina couldn't have witnessed it herself," said Pixley. "But I did. And although I also have a vivid imagination, it's rarely paranoid."

"Agreed," said Ruby. "Talking of paranoid, isn't it a possible side effect of heroin use?"

"Indeed it is," said Niall. "If Luca was in a paranoid state and believed Fina was trying to harm him, he might become aggressive."

"Of everyone on this cursed island, why the deuce would Luca think Fina wanted to harm him?" asked Pixley.

Flora leapt up out of her seat. "I've got it!" She began to pace, clearly recreating the scene in her head. "As I stepped onto Mr Tremore's ferry, Ruby was handing around bits of chocolate. And Mr Tremore told Fina not to give any to his dog, right?"

With a sharp intake of breath, Ruby said, "And Fina said, 'Chocolate is my drug of choice'."

"Spot on," I breathed. "Was that enough for Luca? That's terribly paranoid indeed."

Niall stretched out his legs and tapped his feet together. "If Luca hadn't had his 'fix' given the long journey to Cornwall, it might have made him more sensitive. Or perhaps he was trying to quit and was going into a withdrawal stage."

My shoulders lowered. "That's a weight off my mind. At least one mystery is solved."

Pixley smirked. "And only one left to go, Red."

"Surely this eliminates Luca as a suspect, doesn't it?" asked Flora. "How could a heroin user plan all of these daring crimes?"

"Don't forget he's run a successful gallery whilst being just such an addict," said Pixley.

Niall steepled his fingertips. "Mr Hayford is correct. If a heroin user has a regular supply, they can function for years."

"And couldn't the heroin make him even more focused on his business?" asked Ruby.

"If he managed it correctly, yes." Niall crossed his legs. "I've had a few patients in high-pressure careers who've used it for years. I cannot convince them it will eventually take its toll."

Whilst everyone was talking, Flora shook her head. "I simply don't buy it. Focus, yes, but this level of planning?" She turned to me. "And if he did push Fina, he wasn't managing all that well."

Ruby held out her hands in a wide, appealing gesture. "Let's take a step back. We need to see the big picture before we put the puzzle pieces together."

Pixley pulled up a trouser leg and leaned forward. "And what is the big picture? Forgery? Espionage? Lust?"

"On our first day, you might recall John Benbow uttering a curious phrase."

We all sat in silence, as if we were pupils wrestling with a maths question.

Pixley snapped his fingers. "Parlour games."

"Yes!" chirped Flora. "He said Sir Montague was fond of parlour games."

"And was Sir Montague fond of parlour games, Flora?" Ruby's eyes sparkled.

"How should I know?"

"Didn't you visit Serpentine Hall last year?"

"Well, yes." She paused. "We played squeak piggy squeak."

"And the relevance to the murders is?" asked Charles, a mite testily.

"In detective stories, the victim's character is vitally important. That's where I began, assuming Sir Montague was the intended victim."

"You mean the intended victims could have been John or Helen?" I asked.

"Possibly. For example, John could have technically died before Sir Montague. But I didn't know that for certain, so I focused on Sir Montague and the contest this weekend. It resembles a parlour game, doesn't it?"

"It's rather farcical, now you mention it," said Niall.

Ruby stopped her pacing. "Farcical describes it well, doesn't it, Flora?"

30

"Say nothing, Flora," said someone behind me.

Gwendolyn advanced on our small group in a long black dressing gown, like a high priestess preparing for a ritual sacrifice. She held her head high as she sat next to Flora on the sofa, staring straight ahead at Ruby.

Ruby ran a fingertip along the edge of the mantel. "Who thought of it first? Was it Sir Montague, Flora, or Gwendolyn?"

Flora smirked. "What are you talking about, dear Ruby?"

"You not only planned this contest, but you also planned the little charade in the gallery," said Ruby. "Fina helped you by thinking the candle was dynamite."

Gwendolyn's taut body sagged, and she held her hands up to each cheek like a pantomime of woe. "It was Flora's idea. She always was the most enterprising."

Flora's upper lip curled in a snarl. "What do you mean, Gwenny? It was your idea. You're the one with a low enough opinion of humanity to concoct such a scheme."

"Please." Charles flung out a hand. "We're all familiar enough with the mock surprise game. Too cliched for words."

Ignoring the interruption, Flora said, "Why did you think I proposed the contest? Sir Montague told me it was your idea."

Gwendolyn's eyes rolled upward. "Oh my. We've been had."

"Let me guess," said Ruby. "Sir Montague told Flora it was Gwendolyn's idea and vice versa."

"Jupiter's teeth!" cried Pixley. "The old devil put them up to it?"

Charles scooted to the edge of his chair. "So Gwendolyn and Flora murdered Sir Montague when they learned the truth."

With her hand over her eyes, Flora mumbled, "All right. Sir Montague visited me a few months ago and said Gwendolyn's career had faltered, so we'd use this stunt to drum up publicity for both of us. My career was taking off, and this would add fuel to the fire. It appealed to my competitive streak."

"That doesn't mean you didn't skewer the old man," said Pixley.

"Your story is consistent with your personality, Flora," I said. "But it's not consistent that you'd believe Gwendolyn cooked up this sort of scheme."

"Ah, you don't know Gwendolyn. When her back is in the corner, she'll fight like an alley cat. When we were students, I remember we couldn't pay for dinner one night at a restaurant. Instead of offering to wash dishes or casually skipping the bill, she concocted this elaborate plot to make the waiter believe we had already paid."

Charles drummed his fingers on his knee. "If anything, this gives Flora and Gwendolyn more of a motive. Once they discover they've been had, they fly into a rage and kill him."

Ruby held out a hand to Charles. "Would you help me with a demonstration?"

"Certainly, dear lady." He sprung to his feet.

"Now, whilst Charles is not as tall as Sir Montague, he's the tallest among the guests. So we'll use him as a stand-in for our demonstration.

"When we found Sir Montague's body, it was clear from the tiny larder and the position of the murder weapon at the back of his neck," she said, touching the top of Charles's spine, "that the murderer had to have been nearly embracing Sir Montague from behind."

Ruby slid her arms along either side of Charles and moved closer.

"You can murder me any time, dear lady," he said.

Good Lord. What an oaf.

Saying nothing, Ruby let her arms drop. "Feens, would you assist me?"

Ever ready to help, I sprung up.

"Take my position, would you?"

I did as I was told. Charles's aftershave was rather overpowering, but I stood in place with my arms outstretched.

"Fina, Gwendolyn, and Flora are all petite." Ruby lifted my arm towards Charles's neck. "From their position, it's a nearly impossible angle to thrust a skewer into his neck."

"What about a woman scorned and all that?" asked Pixley.

I glared at him.

"Even if they were in a fury, it's still unlikely," said Ruby.

As I wrinkled my nose at the aftershave smell, I realised we'd already dismissed this theory of the murder. Wasn't Sir Montague killed in the studio, not the larder? Why was Ruby discussing the wrong theory?

A glance at Pixley's frowning face confirmed he was thinking the same thing.

"So you're saying it had to have been me, Charles, Mr Benbow, or Daphne," said Niall.

"You're all about the right height."

"Well, let's get on with it," said Charles. "Tell me, dear Ruby, why I'm the murderer."

Ruby said, "You're a spy for Her Majesty's Government, not an employee of a sugar company."

Charles waved his cigarette. "This is most intriguing. Do tell us more."

"Wait," said Niall. "Before we continue, I need a drink. May I interest anyone else?"

Only Pixley and Charles nodded. "Make mine a neat whisky," said Pixley.

"I'll have the same," said Charles.

Niall dutifully poured the drinks and handed them around.

Despite his nonchalant air, Charles downed the golden liquid in one gulp. "Someone overheard my chat with Sir Montague in the conservatory, didn't they?"

"Actually, it was me," I said. "You forced Sir Montague to host this weekend gathering. The hope was you'd identify a spy on behalf of striking workers in St Lucia, and the Caribbean more broadly."

I paused, waiting for my words to take effect.

Charles had merely closed his eyes, as if that might protect him against my words. So I continued. "Daphne's name was mentioned given her outspoken political views and ample bank account."

Charles's whisky glass slipped to the floor. His eyes remained shut.

"Don't tell me he also takes drugs," said Pixley.

But Niall was already at Charles's side, lifting one eyelid and taking his pulse. He hung his head, sending his unruly mop of hair flopping over.

Flora put her hand over her mouth. "Is he dead?"

"No, thank God. Just sedated. If it's phenobarbital, it acts rapidly." He picked up the whisky glass and held it to the firelight. "There's a bit of residue on this glass."

We all stared at each other in horror. The comfortable storytelling had offered a sense that a tidy solution was coming, and even that there might really be a madman roaming about the island. Not that they were sitting in this cosy room with us right now.

Ruby pointed to a sofa in the corner. "Should we lay him down over there?"

Without waiting for an answer, she approached Charles and lifted his legs, whilst Niall cradled Charles's head and shoulders. When they settled him on the sofa with a blanket, I was almost jealous of his enviable oblivion. Sleep was preferable to constant worry.

Gwendolyn rasped, "What are you going to do now, Miss Dove?"

Even the unflappable Ruby Dove was momentarily defeated. She pulled a hand slowly over her face.

But then she squared her shoulders and marched over to an occasional table overlaid with gleaming obsidian. Thrusting her hand into her bag, she produced the paint tubes we'd used in Mr Benbow's room to discuss our deductions.

"Really, Ruby," said Flora. "This is no time for games. Or are you going to paint us a picture of the murderer?"

"In a manner of speaking, yes." She lined up the tubes on the mantel. "Let's engage in a little psychotherapy of our own, shall we?"

She turned to Pixley and me. "Would you be my assistants?"

Gwendolyn crossed her arms. "Are you leaving yourselves out of the suspect list?"

Flora put in, "It's a pointless exercise if you're not included."

"If and when it's necessary, I will. But for now, let's focus on the victims and most-likely suspects. Now, we've already established Sir Montague's enjoyment of parlour games."

Pixley held up the orange tube of paint.

"Sir Montague's Chrome Orange represents playful mischievousness but also ambition. Clearly, he was an ambitious and successful character," said Ruby.

She pointed at the tube of Cobalt near me, and I held it aloft.

"John Benbow's blue colour represents loyalty, service, and a steady character."

"Poor John," said Flora in a quiet voice. It sounded genuine. Of course, it might have been genuine remorse for murdering him.

"Yes, John Benbow was a steadfast ally and friend to Sir Montague," said Ruby. "They served together in the Great War, and Mr Benbow would do anything to protect and defend his friend."

"So John's loyalty might have got him killed," said Pixley.

"It is possible John was the intended target, though it's unlikely." Ruby nodded at me.

I held up the next logical option: Viridian Green.

"Next, we have Helen Poole," said Ruby. "Mr Benbow thought she was angling to become Lady Montague."

"I had the same impression when I visited last year," said Flora. "And Sir Montague sang her praises, too."

"Yes, we don't know if he was in love with her," said Ruby. "Regardless, he clearly had affection for her."

I was about to say, "Despite her cooking," but thought better of it.

"Helen was one cool customer," said Pixley. "Sharp, efficient, organised, and also mysterious. She was at the top of my suspect list." He paused. "That is until ..."

"She certainly had a motive, which would logically extend to killing John if he suspected her," said Ruby. "But as Pixley says, she was also murdered."

I tapped the Viridian tube against my cheek. "Why did Helen lock me in with the paintings? Her laugh was so devious and unhinged."

"Ah yes, the paintings. Forgery, St Lucia, and perhaps most importantly, Luca."

Ruby suddenly grabbed a nearby water jug. She marched towards Luca and poured it over his head.

31

"Steady on, Ruby," said Pixley. "The poor chap will freeze."

Niall nodded at Ruby. "Well done. Otherwise, she'd need to slap him awake."

As if to prove his point, Luca's blond eyelashes blinked. He shook his body like a dog coming in from the rain. "What happened? Why am I wet?"

Flora handed Luca a blanket. "Here, wipe yourself down. You took too much hard stuff and drifted off."

He worked his jaw. "What are you talking about?"

Niall held up a hand. "We know, Mr Gatti. Time to come clean about your proclivities. Including forgery."

Luca crossed his arms and remained silent.

"Flora first mentioned the possibility of forgery," said Ruby. "It's a curious fact given the scene Fina witnessed."

Taking the cue, I said, "On my way to fetch a snack in the kitchen, I spotted a light in the studio. When I peered through the crack in the door, I spotted Sir Montague, Flora, and Luca all discussing a beautiful portrait of a coal miner. They agreed that no one would ever find out about the painting. I don't have a clue what that meant."

"Later," said Pixley, "we found a photograph of the portrait. The painting's signature read 'Wenna', which Fina cleverly remembered was a Cornish saint."

"And then Pixley realised that 'Wenna' sounded like 'Gwen'," I said.

"We can explain," said Luca. "It's not what you think."

"He's right," said Flora. "Believe it or not, Sir Montague painted the portrait."

Flora stretched her neck from side to side. "We had a plan, meant to be a surprise. Gwendolyn's career might gain speed if she had new paintings under a different name—"

"Like an author with two pen names," said Luca.

"Yes," continued Flora. "And Sir Montague's gift was to paint this series to generate sales and publicity. Gwendolyn is excellent at mimicking styles, so we thought she could copy Sir Montague's style if the plan worked."

"Half a mo," said Pixley. "This was all to help Gwendolyn? You didn't have any ill intent?"

Flora and Luca shook their heads.

"But Gwendolyn was aware of the contest?" asked Pixley.

"Oh yes," said Gwendolyn.

"This also explains why Flora didn't want to meet Gwendolyn and Charles during lunch on that first day," said Ruby. "At first, I thought it was because of Charles, but later it became clear she was nervous that she'd slip up at this first meeting between them."

"It's hard for me to keep a secret," said Flora. "Not because I'd blurt anything, but I have a terrible poker face."

"So you pretended to be highly competitive with Gwendolyn. You used every opportunity to insult her," said Ruby.

Gwendolyn wiped her spectacles. "Flora did a marvellous job. All I had to do was react to her barbs and insults."

"It's a touching story," I said. "But what about the secret

room with the paintings? And why on earth did Helen lock me in?"

Flora said, "It was a convenient spot to lock you in – for whatever deranged reason Helen might have had. Perhaps she thought you had discovered our little scheme."

Pixley squeezed my hand. "Don't think about it, Red."

I patted my pocket, suddenly remembering the little envelope that had fallen out of the painting in the secret room.

Blast it. I'd left the envelope in my other frock upstairs. "I found something, but I don't have it with me. Would you all wait here?"

"Shouldn't someone go with you, Fina?" asked Niall.

∽

"Right behind you, Red," said Pixley as we crested the top of the stairs.

"I can take care of myself," I said.

"Don't be foolish. No one is safe from this lunatic."

"The lunatic is in the drawing room with everyone else," I said.

"It could be Daphne," he said.

"She could be an accomplice, yes. Don't forget that someone in the drawing room drugged Charles."

"You have a point there."

"And who would do that except the murderer?"

"Still, we need to be careful."

I froze. "Did you hear that?"

We switched off our torches, straining our ears in the silence. The wind had given us a momentary reprieve.

Pixley held up a finger. The creaking was moving closer.

Something tickled my leg. With trembling fingers, I fumbled with the torch, training it on my feet.

"Good Lord," breathed Pixley. "It's just that devilish kitten."

After giving Tangerine a squeeze and a nudge, we reached my bedroom. "It's probably better if you keep watch."

He crossed his arms, his stocky figure blocking the door.

I groaned. "The light won't switch on."

"The storm took care of all that," said Pixley. "Just leave the door open. I'm sure there's light from the corridor."

Light, my foot. On tiptoes, I scurried blindly across the floor. What if Daphne were hiding, ready to spring on me?

Focus, Fina. I crept over to the tallboy looming like an ogre in the darkness. Within a minute, I'd found the frock and groped for the packet. Just as I suspected. The envelope wasn't flat, and clearly held sand or powder.

Still fumbling in the darkness, I found the flap on the tiny envelope. Using my fingernail like a paperknife, I slit it open.

"I found it, Pix," I called out.

The light from the corridor shifted, throwing the room into total darkness.

"Pix! I can't see!"

Silence.

Adrenaline flooded my arms and legs.

"Pix?"

Shuffling noises came from the corridor.

I backed further into my room, bumping into the tallboy.

"Fina? Are you in there? I can't see anything, darling. Do turn on the light."

32

Daphne aimed a tiny pistol at my head.

"That's right, darlings, nothing will happen to Fina. If you stay put."

After finding me in my room, Daphne had frog-marched me downstairs and into the drawing room. Pixley had stumbled down the stairs in front of me, rubbing his head from Daphne's assault on his thankfully thick skull.

"You'll never get away with this, Daphne," Pixley said defiantly.

"You parrot the pictures well, but it won't do you any good," she said.

Daphne still wore the clinging yellow gown she'd put on earlier, though the hem was caked with bits of clay and mud. A twig dangled from her blonde hair.

Her pistol waved me into the corner where everyone else had huddled, save for Charles slumbering on a sofa.

Daphne threw back her head and thrust out her bosom. She had one hand on the gun and the other on her hip. "I expect you're all wondering why I have this pistol—"

"Come now, Daphne, it's hopeless. There's no way out."

Why was Luca provoking her?

"Do tell us, Daphne," said Ruby. "Please."

"Ah, dearest Ruby. Ever the clever one, aren't you? Too clever by half. Well, I'm not going to kill you all, so you can relax."

We did. I'd never witnessed such a collective sigh of relief in all my life.

"Now," she said, scratching her cheek with the gun before levelling it at us again. "You're probably wondering why I'm still pointing a gun at you."

"It did cross my mind, yes," said Pixley.

"Well done, Mr Journalist. You see, as I know I'm not the murderer, it's best I keep an eye on all of you until the police arrive."

"You mean we'll sit here until they arrive? If they arrive?" asked Flora.

"If that's what it takes, yes."

"There's no point, Daphne," said Niall quietly. "I've already taken care of it."

Daphne stood on her toes. "Where is he?"

"Who?" asked Gwendolyn. "Do you mean Charles? He's been drugged and is sleeping on the sofa." She pointed behind her.

My stomach clenched. "Did you say you'd 'taken care of it', Niall?"

He dug his nails into the chair. "I drugged Charles. I knew he was the murderer, and I wasn't taking any chances."

"Why not tell us instead?" asked Flora.

Ruby leaned forward. "Shall I tell them, Niall?"

Daphne's gun wavered. "How is it possible? How could you know?"

Ruby sailed across the room like the *Queen Mary*. Then she placed her hand on Daphne's arm. "Put the gun down, for heaven's sake. You'll hurt yourself, or one of us."

Daphne whispered to her, as if none of us could hear. "But they'll go to the police, and then we'll be done for."

"It's possible but doubtful. All that's on our minds is to survive. I expect we'll all want well clear of everything associated with Serpentine Hall as soon as possible."

Inch by inch, Daphne's arm drifted downward, her bangles jingling in a pathetic parody of their usual jolly sound.

Niall rubbed his forehead. "Shall I begin?" He paused. "Actually, Miss Dove, would you mind? It might be better this way."

The wind buffeted the windows, sending streams of cold air through the cracks. I grabbed a blanket and put it around my shoulders. My arms and legs tingled. Just when I thought more revelations couldn't affect me, this confirmation of Daphne and Niall's relationship sent me reeling.

Ruby smoothed her hair and skirt, still standing next to Daphne. She neatly slipped the tiny pistol from Daphne's red-nailed fingertips and stowed it in her pocket.

"I expect Daphne and Niall met through Niall's practice. Is that correct?"

"Quite correct," he said. "But our relationship began after I was no longer seeing her as an official patient."

"What relationship?" I asked, unable to help myself.

Pixley patted my hand.

Niall twisted his lips. "Ah, I see what you're after, Miss Aubrey-Havelock. No, not that type of relationship. More of an alliance, if you will. Mind you, if anyone asked if she was still my patient, we would say 'yes'. It was a useful cover."

"Cover?" asked Pixley.

"The alliance you speak of is a political one, isn't it?" asked Ruby.

"Yes, but I'd rather not discuss the details."

"Why not?" asked Luca, his jaw working overtime. "Why are you special?"

"Let's just say they're working on a series of international campaigns," said Ruby.

"Bolshies, you mean," said Gwendolyn.

"You can call them whatever you like," said Ruby. "The point is, they viewed this weekend as an opportunity for mundane work on these campaigns."

Daphne pushed a strand of hair behind her ear. "Perfectly accurate, Ruby, darling. Mundane is the word, though I did get a bit of a thrill from it all. All the secrecy, I mean. And I do love money flowing to a worthy cause."

"How did you know, Miss Dove?" asked Niall.

"You two were using every opportunity to meet. And though Daphne is dramatic by nature, even her enthusiasm about you seemed a shade overdone. Daphne also made sure you were invited as a judge this weekend, and Sir Montague was happy to play along given his orders from Charles Vane."

"What about the blank piece of paper in Daphne's typewriter?" I asked. "The one Niall took."

As ever, Ruby was prepared. "Pix, might I borrow your lighter?"

He leapt up, presenting her with his silver lighter.

She withdrew a crumpled sheet from her pocket and held it a few inches above the open flame.

33

Ruby held up the paper, now covered in brown script.

"Is it invisible ink?" breathed Flora.

"Yes. I expect it's lemon juice," said Ruby.

My mind flashed with an image of Daphne's room. And that bowl of lemons next to her typewriter.

Pixley snapped his fingers. "The lemon-juice spies! Of course."

"The lemon-juice what?" asked Flora.

"During the Great War, a couple of German spies were caught using the outdated technique of lemon juice to send secret messages. The poor fellows were executed in the Tower of London."

"But this gives Dr Rafferty and Miss Wandesford perfect motives to murder Sir Montague if they're Bolshie spies. And if Sir Montague was a spy."

"I'd say it gives them perfect motives to murder Charles Vane," said Flora. "What would murdering Sir Montague accomplish?"

"And why would I have just given Ruby the gun?" Daphne put in.

Luca threw up his hands. "Fine." He pointed at the sofa where Charles still slept. "Then it gives Charles the perfect motive. Perhaps Sir Montague wanted to quit, or perhaps he threatened to expose Charles."

In the excitement of these revelations, my blanket had slipped from my shoulders. So, too, had my jumper. I picked up the jumper, sending the packet I'd found behind the painting to the floor.

With lightning speed, Gwendolyn scooped it up. "What's this?"

Instead of handing it back to me, she tore it open.

I'd completely forgotten why I went upstairs in the first place.

"Give it to me." I snatched back the envelope from Gwendolyn, spraying the floor with its contents.

Pixley fell to his knees and stuck his nose near the brown powder. Then he dipped his finger in and tasted it. He sat back on his haunches. "It's heroin. Or opium. Hard to tell the difference."

No wonder Luca had suddenly become so loquacious. He was eager to divert attention from himself.

"I found that in the secret room," I said. "It had fallen from one of the paintings."

"Strangely enough, Luca's earlier insistence about us being wrong about forgery was actually truthful," said Ruby. "We were wrong. And that's where you made the mistake, Luca. If you had simply denied it, I wouldn't have concluded you were involved in illegal activities – other than forgery. Your erratic behaviour indicated drugs. Whilst most drug smugglers are rarely addicts themselves, you defy that rule. Maybe the pressure of the London art world made heroin an easy solution."

Luca hung his head but said nothing.

"Given this poor chap's addled state," said Pixley, "he must have needed help. Was Helen the one who helped him?"

"Indeed. I suspected the two were involved either romantically or otherwise, and their connection was only confirmed when we found out they were half-siblings."

Gwendolyn and Flora began talking at once. Flora held up a steadying hand. "And I thought Gwen and I had the biggest secrets this weekend."

Niall raised a finger. "Let me understand: Luca and Helen had a drug-smuggling operation? They stuffed drugs in between the canvases and the frames of paintings Luca sold in his gallery?"

Shivering, Gwendolyn said, "Then we're accessories? Will we go to prison?"

I was rather sorry for Gwendolyn at that moment. She had a mind that jumped to the worst possible conclusion, much like mine.

"We're obviously not the police," said Pixley, "so no one can give you any assurances. But I'm confident your paintings weren't the only ones involved in this scheme."

Flora leapt up and grabbed Luca, shaking his limp body. "Tell us, tell us everything now, Luca!"

His eyelids flickered, and I wondered if he was faking unconsciousness. Flora flung him back into his seat, and his eyes opened.

"You'd better tell us everything," said Ruby. "The police are keen to suspect anyone connected to drugs for murder. And your accomplice is dead, which makes matters even worse for you."

"And you had a splendid motive to murder Sir Montague if he discovered your little operation," said Niall.

Daphne held a hand up to her mouth. "Just like in the films!"

"All right," said Luca. "Curse you if you're trying to pin the murder on me. When I met Helen, she needed money desperately. I did, too. The gallery was failing and I could feel the rising tide of debt. I was up to my neck in it."

He grabbed a nearby glass of water with trembling fingers. "An artist friend had a sideline selling cocaine, and I joked with Helen about how all our troubles would be over if we sold drugs."

"Helen didn't take it as a joke, did she?" asked Ruby.

He massaged the back of his neck. "She'd become bitter about the world, and this scheme offered a twisted revenge on it. My gallery was failing because I didn't have the brain Helen had: a calculating business brain." He chuckled. "I loved art and thought that was enough. I'd never be able to pull off a smuggling scheme on my own."

"When did you start taking drugs?" asked Pixley.

"The money was rolling in and everything was running smoothly. I won't pretend I'm an ethical person, but the whole charade depressed me. That's when I turned to heroin. Ironically, once I did that, my ability to focus – which was already my saving grace – was extraordinary, and the gallery business began to thrive."

"And you wanted out, didn't you?" asked Flora quietly.

He held up his hands in surrender. "God help me, I did. Helen wouldn't hear of it, of course. She said that if I pulled out, she'd expose me."

"Wouldn't she be implicated too?" asked Niall.

"She said no one would believe me if I said she was involved. After all, she was a housekeeper, not a gallery owner."

"Helen was a clever one," said Ruby. "She dropped that glass bowl of custard because Charles's words about people pretending to be someone else caught her on the hop. But she covered that mistake by implying there had been peculiar accidents during the past week. Remember, she was the only one who put that idea into our heads. According to Fina, she even put it in John Benbow's head."

"Just a minute," said Pixley. "John Benbow said Helen had been complaining of these accidents before she dropped the bowl. Why did she invent the lie in the first place?"

"I expect Luca's erratic behaviour was becoming a liability," said Ruby.

"No!" Luca pressed his hands against his ears. "She wouldn't do that. She wouldn't make me have an 'accident'."

"Helen was ruthless, Luca," said Ruby quietly. "You know it's true."

I bounced in my seat. "But was Sir Montague aware of or involved in this scheme?"

"It's possible but unlikely," said Luca. "Though he was fond of parlour games, he had a natural abhorrence of drugs."

Gwendolyn clicked her tongue. "Drugs are part of the art world. I once overheard him yelling at a young artist who also took opium. He stopped working with this student because of it."

"So Helen did this behind Sir Montague's back?" I asked. "And hid the paintings with the drugs in that secret room?"

"I'm certain Helen thought she had hidden it from Sir Montague, but that phone number we found in his pocket was suggestive," said Ruby.

"The Southampton number?" I asked.

Pixley slapped his knee. "Southampton. Of course. Such a major port is a perfect place for the illicit drugs trade. That's why he had the phone number?"

"A likely scenario," said Ruby. "Or perhaps John Benbow gave him the number. I can just imagine Mr Benbow discovering what Helen was up to – since he didn't trust her anyway – and then giving Sir Montague the telephone number to confirm his suspicions."

"Possibly, very possibly," said Luca.

"John didn't trust Helen," I said, "but I assumed it was because she was angling to become Lady Montague. Perhaps it was also this drug operation."

Pixley scratched his head. "What about that invoice we found in John's room? For the coal miner portrait. Why was money changing hands if it was a surprise for Gwendolyn?"

"We did have invoices for all the paintings used in the scheme, of course," said Luca. "But I haven't a clue about that one."

"What if Helen created a bill simply because she wasn't aware of the plan Flora, Luca, and Sir Montague had?" Ruby turned to Luca. "Did Helen know about your little plot?"

"To be honest, I never told her. It slipped my mind. Or rather, the drugs made my mind slip."

"So John Benbow might have had the invoice in his room precisely because he suspected some funny business?" asked Flora.

"That's my guess," said Ruby. "And once Sir Montague and John Benbow turned up dead, Miss Helen Poole realised her goose was well and truly cooked. She couldn't rely on Luca for help, so she began tidying up loose ends, probably beginning by searching John's room for any incriminating evidence related to the smuggling operation."

"Wait a moment," I said, my head spinning. "Helen was asleep when all this happened. Then she awakes and uses the opportunity to put me in that room. Are you saying she was going to kill me?"

"Whether Helen was actually unconscious, I doubt we'll ever know," said Ruby.

Pixley snapped his fingers. "I just thought of something. A magician once showed me a magic trick that makes it look like your pulse has disappeared. You put something like a tennis ball in your armpit, and then you squeeze it. It will make your heart look like it's slowed."

Ruby nodded. "That might explain it. Either way, imagine her state when she awoke if she were asleep all that time. Something dramatic and dreadful has occurred, but she doesn't know what it is. So when everyone leaves the house, except for you, Feens, she sees it as an opportunity. She must hide their operation."

"She needs a free hand, so she locks up Fina whilst she goes about searching John's room and probably burning incriminating papers in the fireplace," said Pixley.

"Yes." I tapped my foot. "Was she going to kill me after that?"

"It's possible, Feens. But it's more likely she'd have just left you there, perhaps until she could make her getaway. It was her only chance."

34

A gust of wind blew open one of the French windows. With one voracious blast, the wind extinguished the fire.

Pixley stretched and rose. "You all carry on. I'll restart the fire." He reached back and scooped up his jacket. "I say, has anyone seen Charles?"

"He's scarpered," said Luca.

Flora and I ran to the windows, scanning the horizon. But it was so dark it looked as if the windows were painted black.

"I can't understand it," said Niall. "The sedative I gave him can't have worn off that quickly."

"Charles is a professional, remember," said Pixley. "He probably made us think he was drinking the whisky."

I surveyed the chair he'd been sitting in before he fell asleep. "Notice those brown stains on his chair? He probably poured his whisky on the cushions."

"The devil," said Pixley.

"Taking my name in vain again," came a voice from the doorway.

Charles's eyes twinkled. "Though it pained me to ruin a beautiful antique, my self-preservation was more important than Sir Montague's furniture. Furniture he will no longer enjoy."

Niall's finger quivered as he pointed at Charles. "You're the reason he won't be able to enjoy anything. You're the murderer."

That self-satisfied smirk grew even stronger. "If so, prove it." He turned to Ruby. "Or better yet, I want to hear your theories."

"There are too many people milling about, making me nervous," said Gwendolyn. "Could we all sit down?"

"I agree," said Flora. "And while we're at it, who has Daphne's gun?"

Ruby patted her pocket. "Gwendolyn and Flora are right. Let's all sit down, shall we?" She sat on a wooden chair.

Charles and Daphne sloped towards the nearest furniture. Charles melted into a chair, still with his devil-may-care attitude, whilst Daphne sat on the edge of a settee.

Luca glanced at Charles. "Only a murderer could be so relaxed."

"As I recall, dear boy, you were rather relaxed in your chair for a good forty minutes," Charles retorted.

Luca rose from his seat, but Ruby held up a forestalling hand. "Charles is the only person we haven't subjected to scrutiny."

"You can subject me to scrutiny any day, Ruby Dove."

"Pipe down, Charles," growled Pixley.

"Thank you, Pix. Now, Mr Charles Vane was the unknown quantity this weekend."

"Hence Helen's choice of Zinc White for his room," I said.

"Precisely. No one knew why he was a judge or who he worked for."

"He was Gwendolyn's judge, though," said Niall.

Gwendolyn coughed. "Sir Montague suggested him. I hadn't any better ideas, so I went along with it."

"Wouldn't that have put you at a disadvantage?" asked Daphne.

"That was the first sign of a major inconsistency this weekend," said Ruby. "Why would Gwendolyn agree to an unknown judge?"

Pixley snapped his fingers. "Because the contest was a fake, so it didn't matter anyway."

Gwendolyn nodded.

"How does this implicate Charles?" asked Flora.

"Well, Sir Montague invited Charles, and Charles also had a hold over him. We also know Charles is a spy for the British Government, or the local government in Barbados."

Charles kept his smirk but said nothing.

"What about his conversation with you about sketching? And his claim to be Ian Clavering's half-brother?" I asked.

"Who is Ian Clavering?" asked Gwendolyn.

Ruby shot me a warning look. Clearly, I should have left out the Ian portion of the question.

"As to the sketching, I believe that was genuine. But about Ian Clavering – my friend with a striking resemblance to Charles – it's impossible they're related."

"How can you be so certain?" Pixley asked. "The likeness is remarkable."

"When I mentioned that I'd seen the great Pan-Africanist Marcus Garvey speak, Charles said he'd never heard of him. Now, anyone associated with Ian would have heard of Marcus Garvey. More than that, if he'd ever read a newspaper in the past ten years, he would have recognised his name."

"So he must have been lying," I said.

"But why?" asked Pixley. "If he was pretending to be Ian's half-brother, why say something that so obviously makes it implausible?"

"Probably to confuse me." Ruby was pacing in front of the

fire, turning on her heel like a general inspecting the troops. "And it worked. I was completely at sea. Pardon the pun."

With rising irritation, I said, "Why are you smirking, Charles?"

He flicked a speck of dust from his trousers. "Watching Miss Dove tie herself up in knots over a chap like Marcus Garvey is amusing. Most amusing."

"What does this matter, dear Ruby?" asked Daphne. "He's obviously the murderer. Sir Montague was going to expose him or give away state secrets, so he killed him."

Ruby halted and stared into the fire. Without turning to us, she murmured, "It would be convenient. But Charles isn't the murderer."

35

The makeshift lamp cast a weak light into the larder, illuminating hard, stale bread loaves and a few wilted vegetables.

Charles lit a cigarette. "I'm glad to be cleared of murder, but is this drama necessary?"

"A demonstration is the only way to explain." Ruby pointed her toe at the sacks on the floor. "At first, we all thought that this was the scene of the crime."

"Why at first?" asked Flora. "Isn't that how it happened?"

"Two points didn't make sense. First, there wasn't enough blood on the floor, and second, we found blood in Sir Montague's studio."

"Bloody hell!" cried Luca. "You're saying the killer dragged Sir Montague across the great hall and down the stairs? How would that be possible, and why?"

"That's precisely the problem." Ruby tapped her feet. "Too many people were roaming about when he was murdered. Besides, we would have spotted trails of blood somewhere along the way."

"Could they have dragged the body outside?" asked Pixley.

"It's more plausible," said Ruby. "But you'd still need to enter the front door."

"There would be mud on the body," said Daphne.

"The killer would also have blood or mud on their clothes," said Ruby.

Pixley snapped his fingers. "I see what you're getting at. Charles has continued to wear his immaculate white robe at every turn."

"He was entering the library before we discovered the body," I said, "and he was wearing his white dressing gown then."

"I've seen him in that dressing gown since then," Pixley put in.

Luca stamped a foot. "You're saying that a dressing gown is his alibi? What if he simply took it off?"

"Possible, but he would have had to retrieve it," said Ruby. "All of this speculation is irrelevant, however."

She turned to Luca. "Because Sir Montague wasn't killed in the studio, was he?"

Luca's mouth dropped open. "What on earth do you mean?"

"You have a cut on your finger. It didn't appear until after the murder."

"So? It's just a paper cut. Everyone has them."

She turned to me. "Feens, how did you cut your finger?"

"I cut myself with a razor. It was on the floor of the secret room, next to that packet of drugs."

Ruby held up a finger. "The pieces fell into place after I heard about the razor. This is what happened: Luca stayed behind after his tête-à-tête with Sir Montague and Flora. He stayed behind to slice the backing of the painting to insert the packet of drugs. That's how they smuggle the drugs."

"How did Fina's razor prompt this discovery?" asked Flora.

"On the desk in the studio, I spotted a paint scraper that

artists use on their canvases. They're so sharp that a painter can often just use a razor instead."

Pixley slapped his knee. "Luca was fiddling with the scraper and cut himself. Hey presto – blood on the desk."

"You're right. It was my blood," said Luca.

"Why didn't you just tell us?" asked Pixley.

"To be honest, I don't remember it," he said. "My memory is a bit foggy at the best of times."

I stared at the snowy flour blanketing the larder. "So he was killed here. The murderer must have hated Sir Montague passionately to kill him with a skewer."

"And yet," said Ruby, "the murderer must have been intimate with Sir Montague. To kill him, they had to put their arms around him."

"Love and hate," breathed Pixley. "Psychology again."

Ruby's eyes flashed. "It's possible that Flora or Gwendolyn could have, but even wearing high heels wouldn't provide the height needed to force a skewer down at that angle."

"It could have been you, Ruby," said Gwendolyn. "With or without high heels."

"It's a ludicrous statement," I spat out. "We've already established she's been witnessed at key moments for all the murders. Besides, what was her motive?"

Charles waved a dismissive hand. "Don't let Gwendolyn distract you, dear Ruby."

Unperturbed, Ruby continued. "Now, Helen Poole was a likely starter, except that she's also dead. The only way that's possible is if she had an accomplice who shot her."

"What if she didn't have an accomplice, but was killed by someone avenging Sir Montague and John's deaths?" asked Flora.

"It's hard to imagine anyone here caring enough about Sir

Montague to commit such a murder. Except for John and Helen, of course."

"Which brings us back to Helen's accomplice. If their plan went pear-shaped, that would explain her death," said Pixley.

"Yes, which also returns us to the issue of keys," said Ruby.

Pixley's eyes zigzagged towards the ceiling. "Gwendolyn or Ruby were the only ones who could have locked Helen in the billiard room."

"And I'd testify that Gwendolyn's condition made that impossible," said Niall.

"And there were witnesses to Ruby's whereabouts," Pixley put in.

"Back to a lone murderer," I said. "It still seems impossible."

Ruby motioned to the floor. "You might wonder why there's flour everywhere."

"Well, yes, and why I found you covered in it," said Charles.

Ruby held up the bullet she'd found. "After Helen's death, we noticed a spot of flour near the body. That led us here, where I found a sack with a bullet hole and a bullet."

Gwendolyn raised her eyebrows. "Helen was shot in the larder and moved to the billiard room? How would the killer have had time? We all came running as soon as we heard the shot."

"Besides, they'd be covered in flour," Daphne said.

"Quite right," said Ruby. "And there's the further complication of this extra bullet, since one must be lodged in the body."

Niall coughed. "So two bullets were fired, but we only heard one shot?"

Everyone murmured agreement about hearing just the one.

"If we all only heard one shot," said Ruby, "then the other was muffled by something. And that something was a sack of flour."

"Wouldn't it create a terrific mess in the billiard room?"

asked Daphne.

"Indeed. What happened is this: the killer heard Helen yelling from her locked bedroom, where Gwendolyn had locked her in, as she told Fina. The walls aren't as thick as Gwendolyn had hoped. So the killer releases Helen from her bedroom, and orders her to meet in the billiard room, probably because that's the only place they won't be disturbed. The murderer also instructs Helen to avoid being seen, though Helen probably would have done that anyway."

"But why would Helen agree?" I asked. "And how did the murderer get the key to release Helen from her bedroom? Only you and Gwendolyn had keys."

"The killer might have threatened Helen, or maybe promised her an escape plan," said Ruby.

Pixley rubbed his forehead. "And then the killer shoots Helen with the sack of flour to muffle the shot in the billiard room. Then they clean up the flour and lock her in that same room. Then what?"

"The killer cleans themselves, because they're covered in flour. This is why the second shot is essential. The murderer needed enough time to clean up the mess and to lock the door. Then it would look like suicide or an impossible locked-room crime. After cleaning themselves, they shoot another sack of flour. They probably stand in the hallway and aim the shot into the larder, avoiding the problem of soiled clothes. Then they pretend to join in with everyone else when they rush downstairs."

"That's a perfectly marvellous deduction, but we still have the perfectly futile problem of the keys," said Pixley.

"When Gwendolyn locked Helen in her bedroom and then rescued Fina, only one other person was in the house. Which means only one person could have heard Helen yelling. And only one person might also have an extra set of keys."

36

"Daphne Wandesford," said Ruby.

With a yelp, Daphne sped through the corridor. She'd changed out of her usual tight-fitting clothes into a pair of elegant yet serviceable trousers, so her long legs carried her at a surprisingly fast clip.

"After her!" Charles sprinted up the stairs.

The rest of our party followed at a slower pace. Since we were on an island, it seemed pointless to rush after her. In fact, I'd rather that Daphne did hide in a cave until the police arrived.

Ruby had the same idea, or at least a refusal to hurry in heels.

"How did you know?" I asked.

Ruby clicked on her torch, and a weak light lit up the earthen path winding away from the house. "The viciousness of the crime suggested a long-standing relationship. Gwendolyn and Flora knew Sir Montague, but they weren't children when they met him. Flora was the only one who might have had an extra set of keys because she had visited Cutmere Perch before. But Flora was simply too short to have murdered Sir Montague."

"So it must've been the old family friend: Daphne."

"Also, remember how Daphne drank only wine at lunch on that first day?"

"It was peculiar. Daphne loves food. She had eaten that sandwich on the boat, though. Perhaps that was enough?"

"I doubt it, especially because she said she was famished, remember? And if she had been a true outsider, it would have been rude to reject lunch."

"Or it meant she knew how dreadful Helen's cooking was!"

In the distance, other torches played against the cloud-covered sky. Daphne was nowhere in sight.

"So Daphne hated Sir Montague. Did he do something to her father? Betray him?"

"Did you notice how alike Sir Montague and Daphne were?"

"Alike? You mean in personality?"

"Partially, yes. It was subtle and meant nothing on its own, but they had voracious appetites, both where food and romantic entanglements were concerned. They both were tall and had enormous hands. Both were dramatic, almost theatrical personalities. And Daphne loved various causes, whilst Sir Montague loved art."

"Surely that's not enough to suspect her."

"No, but it was enough to make me study Daphne more closely. It wasn't a conscious studying of her – more as if my subconscious were watching her. And when we began to discuss Gwendolyn being an orphan, along with Helen and Luca's sibling ties, it all began to fit together."

I gasped. "Sir Montague and Daphne were related?"

"I suspect Daphne is his daughter."

"But Daphne is the heiress to the Wandesford rolling-pin fortune. So she can't be Sir Montague's daughter."

Shrieks and cries echoed across the flat land, mixed with the pounding of the waves. We were closer to the sea now.

Our torchlights jiggled wildly as we dashed towards the

gathering crowd on the clifftop. Their torchlights lit up a figure on a cliff overlooking a small cove.

"Will you just all go away?" Daphne yelled against the increasing wind.

"Don't do it," cried Pixley. "It's not worth it. We know you're a good person. I'm certain there's a reasonable explanation."

Her streaming blonde hair flapped against her face. "No, I'm not a good person. I tried but failed. My drive to do good led me to kill him."

Ruby's heels wobbled on the rocks. "You have a heart, and perhaps a jury will see it. Give them a chance, won't you?"

In one swift movement, Daphne leapt over the cliff.

I shall never forget her scream.

∼

PIXLEY and I hugged each other, and Ruby flung her arms around both of us.

"She's at peace now, she's at peace," Flora intoned.

"Let's all return to the house," Niall said. "There's no point in shivering out here."

My limbs were heavy, and my feet wouldn't move.

"It's the shock," whispered Ruby. "Let's go, Feens."

Everyone drifted like wraiths along the winding path back to the house.

But I stopped.

"Did you hear that?" I spun round and trotted towards the cliff.

"Red! What are you doing?"

"Feens, wait. You'll get hurt."

At the edge, I peered over, training my torchlight on the soft brown sand. The white foam from the sea glowed in the darkness. And something else glowed. It was Daphne's blonde hair.

"It's her!"

Pixley grabbed me from behind.

"Let go! Don't you see?"

Finally, he released my arms and leaned forward.

"Everyone, come quickly!" he cried.

Footsteps rumbled behind us, arriving to discover what I had already seen.

With a triumphant smile, Daphne Wandesford was rowing away in a dinghy.

37

"Is this hole deep enough?"

Raindrops sprinkled my face, cooling my overheated cheeks. I wiped my brow and leaned against my spade, surveying the grey earthworms wriggling free of the sweet-smelling soil. The sky had turned a flat monotone over Ruby's delightful new cottage in Crickle Hythe, a hamlet in the outer orbit of Oxford. Though the front garden looked as though an army of badgers had taken up residence, the honeyed stone cottage with crimson curtains still glowed under a lowering sky.

"Just an inch deeper, Feens, and you'll be finished." Ruby handed me a long-handled shovel. "Use this. It's much easier on your back."

"Humph." The shovel was taller than me, and its rough handle looked like a recipe for splinters. "You lured me here with the promise of tying up loose ends from Cutmere Perch. Instead, I find myself doing hard labour for your blasted vegetable garden."

Ruby pushed back the blue kerchief on her head. "You're understandably irritated with me, but there was a reason I couldn't tell you everything over the telephone. But you're right. It's time for me to tie up those loose ends."

"Lemonade for the lemon sisters!" Ever dapper in a brown worsted suit, Pixley trundled from the cottage, holding a tray of sloshing lemonade glasses.

"Perfect timing, Pix." Ruby set her spade against the hedge. "Lemon sisters is typical Pixley Hayford twaddle, but it does explain what's in my pocket."

"Which is?" The sweet-sour lemonade soothed my scratchy throat.

She handed me a sheet of paper covered in brown handwriting.

"Ah. The lemon-juice trick."

"Great Scott! You don't mean this is a letter from Daphne?" Pixley's finger traced the words on the page. "Why didn't you give it to the police? If they find out …"

"That's why I couldn't discuss it on the telephone. Daphne must have slipped this paper into my pocket before she made her escape. I didn't discover it in my jacket until we'd been let go by the police. The rest is lemon-juice history."

Pixley chuckled. "Of course. Typical and brilliant Miss Dove."

"I'll read the letter aloud," said Ruby.

Dearest friends,

If you're reading this, darlings, I'm quite certain I'm dead or have escaped to a glorious tropical island. Hopefully the latter, but I fear the former is a distinct possibility.

You're wondering why I did it. Unless Miss Ruby Dove is reading this letter because she must already know.

As dear Niall says, so much of our lives unfold in response to our childhood. Dear Niall. He's the reason – or the catalyst – for why this all started. During a painting session with him one day, I realised I wanted to write a memoir.

Though I'm only twenty-eight, I've seen a bit of life. I also knew my spot in the limelight could be put to good use. I'd dovetail my glamorous experiences with a peppering of politics.

With a bit of research, however, my childhood story unravelled. You see, I lived with my mother in Button Lane, Sheffield, until age ten, when she died of the flu. They were happy days, but we barely had two sticks to rub together.

We managed, a feat funded by my absent and mysterious father. When Mum died, Horace Wandesford appeared on our doorstep. He said he was my father and that he'd come to take me away.

He did just that, and I became heiress to the Wandesford rolling-pin fortune. On my twenty-first birthday, Dad died in a boating accident, and I inherited his vast estate.

When I interviewed my father's former valet, he reluctantly told me I wasn't Horace Wandesford's daughter. Sir Montague and my supposed father were close, but I never guessed that Sir Montague was my real father. Horace never married, but he wanted children, so when my mother died, Sir Montague offered me up like a wrapped Christmas package.

All of this would have been dramatic enough, darlings – even for moi – but the delectable icing on the cake was that Horace Wandesford never made a will. He was superstitious and worried that it would cause him to somehow forfeit either his life or his fortune.

You can guess the rest. As I was never officially adopted, I shouldn't have inherited his fortune. I knew it was simply a matter of time before other Wandesford relatives discovered this and contested my inheritance. It's doubtful that the court would rule in my favour.

So here I was, up to my eyeballs in debt for good causes, including funding the scheme to help Gwendolyn by giving Luca money to cover initial costs at the gallery. It was the least of my troubles, as I had already given away thousands of pounds and promised even more.

Now, I'm not one to hold a grudge, but discovering Sir Montague was my father made me rather salty. To put it bluntly, darlings, I was absolutely furious.

So I killed him. No need to pen all the sordid details here. John Benbow guessed it was me, so he also had to go. I am truly sorry about dear John, and would have never killed my father had I realised it would also involve John. Helen thought she could hold it over me for a bit of cash. But she was mistaken.

Don't fret, darlings. I've had a marvellous run, and I've loved every minute.

Yours,
Daphne

Pixley rubbed his smooth head. "Well, I'll be ... I never took Daphne as a serious suspect. Too warm-hearted."

I frowned at Ruby. "But why did you suggest Niall as an accomplice when we were using those paint tubes? Did you really suspect both of them?"

She grimaced. "Whilst I had a strong suspicion of Daphne, I wanted to understand her relationship with Niall. I was confident it didn't involve the murders, but it needed to be tidied before we could move forward."

"Okay, but why didn't you tell us that?" asked Pixley.

She wiped the condensation from her lemonade glass. "Well, I hoped that putting the idea in your heads might lead somewhere."

"So you were using us," said Pixley.

"Pixley Hayford," I said, "she was merely prodding our subconsciouses."

"Thanks, Feens." She sighed. "I didn't know anything for certain, so it was an experiment."

"We did search Daphne's room, so your experiment was successful." I shifted in my seat. "What did that lemon-juice letter actually say?"

She rubbed her eye. "The letter I found and destroyed before the police arrived would have indirectly implicated us. It involved a complex campaign between Irish anti-colonial causes, our Oxford connections, and uprisings in the Caribbean."

Pixley let out a low whistle. "Well done. Even if Niall is in the soup, your plan to keep us safe may work."

I tipped over my lemonade glass. "What do you mean?"

38

Pixley handed me a crumpled newspaper from inside his jacket. "Sorry, Red. I thought you knew."

I mouthed the words: "Harley Street Doctor Caught in Murder Scandal."

Ruby snatched the paper from me. "Don't read the rest, Feens. It will just upset you."

"Give it to me." I held out my hand.

"Really, Red. I'll summarise it for you," said Pixley. "My dear brethren at the *Daily Star* have fixated on implicating Niall in an improper relationship with a client, namely Daphne. Who, of course, remains at large in the Atlantic."

My limbs were stiff with worry. "His career is over. Or at least his career on Harley Street."

"Possibly," said Pixley quietly. "His apparent entanglement with Helen doesn't help, either. Remember how she came to his office to discuss Luca?"

"You mean the invoice without a name on Sir Montague's desk?" I asked.

"The police traced the invoice number to Helen when they searched Niall's office," said Pixley.

My voice rose to a screech. "Are they going to try Niall as an accomplice?"

Pixley stared at his knees. "We don't know, Red. Everything's unresolved until they can locate Daphne."

"Maybe I should call on him? As a friend?" I squeaked.

Ruby looked at Pixley and patted my hand. "You know that will only make matters worse. I'm certain the police are watching us."

Bees buzzed lazily about us. Ruby's fat grey cat, Pasty, was hunting some poor animal under the hedge. This perfect bucolic scene had turned sinister.

Footsteps crunched the pea shingle along the canal path.

∼

"Are you a Miss Ruby Dove? Primrose Cottage?"

A man with a walrus moustache and a vast belly held out a green envelope. His face was a beetroot colour.

Ruby thanked him and opened the envelope.

Pixley watched the postman retreating. "I say, shouldn't he recognise you by now?"

"He's smitten with her," I said.

Ruby shook her head. "Sorry, I can't concentrate. It's a letter from Ian. He's in Barbados, but he read about our case in the papers."

I gulped down my lemonade. "I assume he heard about Charles Vane?"

"It's Ian, so of course it's in code. Let's see. He says that no one named Charles Vane works for Ledburn and Lamport sugar company, nor does he have a relative by that name. He has a cousin who resembles him, but they had a falling out over politics."

"Unsurprisingly, if this so-called Vane chap works for Her Majesty's Government," said Pixley.

"So he was spying on us?" I asked.

"Ian believes it's possible." Ruby looked up. "Fortunately, we didn't fall for his charms."

Pixley wrinkled his nose. "Not to quibble, but you did seem to fall for the fellow."

With a half-smile, she looked from me to Pixley. "You believed my performance? I thought it was rather unconvincing."

He raised his eyebrows. "Performance?"

"You mean you pretended to fall for him, to what – give him a false sense of security?" I asked.

She nodded. "I guessed that click we heard on our telephone call that night to Perry was Charles listening in. To protect us, I continued the farce that I was in love with him. Actually, I expect my subconscious took inspiration from Gwendolyn and Flora pretending to hate each other."

"Well, well. Miss Ruby Dove does it again. You fooled me."

"Will Ian be in London soon?" I asked.

She crumpled the letter. "He doesn't say."

Ruby's cat jumped into Pixley's lap, breaking the awkward silence.

"Hey! Get off, you beast!"

Pasty twitched his tail under Pixley's nose and began kneading his claws on his trousers.

"Here, I'll take the beastie." I scooped him up and placed him on my lap. "He picked you because he knows you don't like cats."

"Well, he's right. He ruined my trousers."

"Oh pish." Ruby leaned towards Pixley. "They're fine. Pasty is the perfect cat."

"What's next? Will you start a zoo, Ruby Dove? I never thought I'd hear you say 'perfect' and 'cat' together," he said.

"Talking of perfect, I still have questions about the disaster named Luca Gatti," I said.

"Good Lord, is he ever," said Pixley.

"Why did he, Flora, and Gwendolyn all throw one another under the proverbial bus?"

Ruby tapped her teeth. "Though Flora and I are not on speaking terms at the moment, I asked her about it before we left the island. She said that whilst she couldn't speak for the others, she believed they all thought they'd distance themselves from each other to avoid revealing the real story behind the contest. I also think Flora panicked at some point, suspecting that Luca was involved in dodgy activities."

"What put you on to Luca and Helen? Did you suspect them of being half-siblings?"

"I definitely had that wrong, though I did suspect they knew each other. Remember when Helen lied about knowing Niall within the first few minutes of us meeting her? That's why I watched her actions rather than listened to her words. In fact, Helen chose our room colours. I had to believe that she knew something about all of us, even if we hadn't met her in person. Then Luca said she'd given him a notebook, and to top it off, he was the one soothing her after her accident. It was all too familiar."

"Helen was a clever clogs, but thoroughly distasteful," said Pixley. "Tell me, was that whole Rip Van Winkle event actually true? Was she drugged?"

"Charles said he didn't give her any pills, but Helen insisted he did. Now, Charles was the most obvious odd man out that weekend, so it would make sense she'd blame him because we'd be likely to believe her. When we tried to wake her, I also noticed that a bit of make-up came off on my finger. At the time, my brain didn't process it, but my subconscious did."

I squeezed Pasty. "That's why you stared at your hand and then rubbed your nose! The famous Ruby Dove tell. But you didn't even know why you'd done it."

"Not at the time, but I began to wonder soon after," said Ruby.

"Why did Helen lie in the first place?" asked Pixley. "Why was she pretending to be asleep?"

"Two possibilities struck me. First, Luca could have told Helen he suspected Fina knew about the drugs. So she might have needed time to think. The accident provided that time, even though I do believe it was a genuine accident. The second possibility was that she interpreted Luca's story about Fina differently. That is, that he was paranoid because of the drugs, which also meant he was a loose cannon. She gained time by pretending to be drugged."

"Phew," said Pixley. "Our intrepid reporter has one more question."

"Why are you referring to yourself in the third person?" I asked.

"Because he's the great and wondrous Pixley." Ruby laughed.

He took a little bow in his seat. "Now. Those blasted papers in John's room. Why was the invoice for the coal miner painting stolen? Who stole the will?"

"The invoice was part of making the Gwendolyn scheme seem like legitimate business. Perhaps they were paying Luca to go along with the fake contest. Either way, I doubt John knew the underlying reason for it all. He struck me as wanting to stay well away from those affairs."

"And the will?" I asked.

"If it was the will that was missing, it must have been

Daphne who took it. Just think: if she were in Sir Montague's will, she'd have a motive."

"Didn't she need the money?" asked Pixley.

"She wouldn't need the money if she could keep up the lie that Horace Wandesford was her father."

"If there's anything that upsets me about all this, it's John," I said, stroking Pasty's head. "He was a sweet soul."

"I should have thought Dr Rafferty would upset you more," said Pixley.

"Pix!" cried Ruby. "Don't be beastly to Feens."

Sighing, I folded my hands in my lap. "I doubt there was ever anything in it."

"Balderdash. Tommyrot," said Pixley. "He was simply gaga over you."

Ruby stared at the sky. "We've all left broken hearts in our wake, haven't we? Every adventure seems to bring a new one."

Pixley snorted. "Especially with you two."

"You're no slouch in that department, Pix," I said.

"Ah yes, there's more herring in the sea," he said.

Ruby waved at the Oxford canal in front of us. "Talking of water, I might take up fishing."

"You?" we said in unison.

"That'll be the day," I said.

"You'll see, Feens. I'm determined to settle down in this cottage, attend to my studies, design clothes, and become a village person."

Pixley grinned. "Well, you're lucky that nothing exciting ever happens in an English village."

The End
Thank you for reading *The Art of Murder!*

Positive reviews help readers discover this book. If you enjoyed *The Art of Murder*, I'd be grateful for a review (Australia, Germany, United Kingdom, or United States).

If you want updates and goodies, please join my reader group!

MORE MYSTERIES

The Ruby Dove Mystery Series follows the early adventures of our intrepid amateur-spy sleuths:

Book 1: The Mystery of Ruby's Sugar
Book 2: The Mystery of Ruby's Smoke
Book 3: The Mystery of Ruby's Stiletto
Book 4: The Mystery of Ruby's Tracks
Book 5: The Mystery of Ruby's Mistletoe
Book 6: The Mystery of Ruby's Roulette
Book 7: The Mystery of Ruby's Mask
Ruby Dove Mysteries Box Set 1
Ruby Dove Mysteries Box Set 2

With many cases under their fashionable belts, Ruby and Fina are ready for more in *Partners in Spying Mysteries:*

Fatal Festivities: A Christmas Novella
Book 1: Death in Velvet
Book 2: The Art of Murder

ABOUT THE AUTHOR

Rose Donovan is a lifelong devotee of golden age mysteries. She now travels the world seeking cosy spots to write, new adventures to inspire devious plot twists, and adorable animals to petsit.

www.rosedonovan.com
rose@rosedonovan.com
Reader Group
Follow me on Bookbub
Follow me on Goodreads

NOTE ABOUT UK STYLE

Readers fluent in US English may believe words such as "fuelled", "signalled", "hiccough", "fulfil", "titbit", "oesophagus", "blinkers", and "practise" are typographical errors in this text. Rest assured this is simply British spelling. There are also spacing and punctuation formatting differences, including periods after quotation marks in certain circumstances.

If you find any errors, I always appreciate an email so I can correct them! Please email me at rose@rosedonovan.com. Thank you!